A PLACE OF BRIGHTNESS

Keith Massey

Lingua Sacra Publishing

A Place of Brightness
Copyright © 2011 by Keith Massey

Published in the United States by Lingua Sacra
Publishing.
www.linguasacrapublishing.com
ISBN 978-0-9843432-0-1

Dedication

To my twin, the Rev. Kevin Massey.

About the Author

Keith Massey, Ph.D., is the author of *Intermediate Arabic for Dummies* and *Next Stop: Spanish.* He is a former linguist with the National Security Agency and is currently a language instructor.

Legal Disclaimer

Chapter One

The spring of 1962 awakens in the area of Brasov, a hundred miles north of Bucharest, the capital of Romania. For fifteen years the "Haiduci" have carried out guerrilla attacks against the Securitaté — the Secret Police of the Communist government. Now, in the final days of this insurgency, a Haiduci family conducts what they hope will be their final mission.

"I hate these moonless nights," Petre said, plodding through the darkness under towering pine trees.

"Look there," his sister Doina said. She raised her walking staff and pointed to their right. "It's rising just now on the horizon."

Petre saw a sliver of silvery light over the distant Carpathian Mountains. "So you inherited our father's eyes as well as his ears," he said. "What magic powers did I get?"

"I can't fire a gun as well as you," she answered.

He laughed. "If you could, you wouldn't need me at all. And the Communists would fall from power in days."

The lights of the city of Brasov dotted the horizon. There, as in all Romania, each apartment building and every place of work had informants who told the Secret Police about any activities deemed dangerous to the

State. Going to Church or reading the wrong books could place one under suspicion of treason.

"I can't do this alone," she said, adjusting the shoulder strap of her AK-47. "Your aim is even better than Grandma's." She smiled in thought. "It's strange how these powers cross between the genders and generations of our family."

Petre took a deep breath and slowly released it. The growing light from the moon illuminated the mist that streamed past his face. "The day you were born Grandma told us about her premonition. She said that your sons would end communism once and for all."

"Maybe your future children could help?" she asked nervously.

Petre stopped walking. "Do you ever just wish we were normal people?"

She continued a few paces forward and turned suddenly to face him; her long black ponytail swirled to land gracefully in front of her tall and svelte frame.

"No!" she exclaimed. "Everyone in the village thinks we're just farmers. But we're members of the Haiduci!"

"That word used to denote bandits and brigands," he said. "I prefer the term 'Freedom Fighter'."

Doina grabbed his shoulder and pulled him forward. "Tell me again how it all started."

Petre laughed and walked with her. "I'm more interested in how it will finally end."

"I want to hear the story again."

"You know it as well as I do."

"But I love the way you tell it," she said seriously.

He smiled and relented. "Long ago, the Turks invaded our land. One of our ancestors began to fight them using a shepherd's skills."

As they continued, Doina picked up a rock from the ground. Peering into the dark forest before them, she hurled it forward. A moment later an explosion of stone on bark echoed back. "You mean like that?"

"Showoff," he said. "So skills with a shepherd's staff and throwing stones were developed and passed down by fathers and mothers to sons and daughters alike. Over time we've added newer weapons. But one thing has never changed. Whenever the sovereignty of Romania is threatened, our family feels the duty to fight."

Petre saw Doina moving her lips along with his practiced words. "After the Turks, we fought the Nazis," he continued. "And today —"

"We face our greatest challenge," she interrupted. "The Communists are more vicious than the Turks ever were. The struggle for our land will take generations." She closed eyes suddenly misting with tears. "We fight for a day when Romania will once again be free."

"You always take over the story at the end," he said.

"Next time I'll let you finish it."

Doina stopped and explored the pockets of her camouflage-patterned coat. "It's time for the pre-attack inventory."

"Right." Petre checked the various pockets in his ragged brown leather coat. "I've got five good throwing stones."

"Same here," she said. "Three loaded clips for a total of ninety rounds. And I have the hunting knife. I'm all set." She placed her weapons carefully on the ground and stretched her arms into the air. As she then reached down to touch her toes, she winced and carefully touched her left side through her heavy jacket.

Her brother noticed. "Are you still in pain?" he asked. "That guard kicked you pretty good last week."

"Last thing he ever did," she said, sitting down on the ground. "It's not so bad. What bothers me is that I'm only twenty years old and already not in the shape I was just two years ago."

"And I'm five years older than you!" Petre gave a last look through his pockets. "Weapons status confirmed," he said, sitting down beside his sister. "Remember what we said, Doinitsa."

"I know. It's our last mission."

"After those recent arrests, the Secret Police have our code names," he said, reaching toward his toes. "If we keep going, they'll eventually figure out who we are."

Doina nodded slowly as she watched him reach for his toes. "Turn to each side a little more," she said. "You always cheat on your stretching."

He complied with her advice and contorted his body. "I'm just not as limber as you," he grunted. "You really think I'll ever have to twist this way in the field?"

"You never know."

Petre stood up slowly. "And also don't forget that we need to settle down and have families ourselves. We can't let this old tradition end with us."

"I notice you've got a prospect in that area," she said, stretching forward and extending her fingers well past her toes. "You and Elena are the talk of the village."

Petre's eyes lit up. "She's an amazing woman."

Doina jumped to her feet. Flinging her rifle over her shoulder, she turned to her brother. "Let's go," she said.

They began to walk.

"What about you?" he asked. "Anyone in the village have your attention?"

"No ..." She closed her eyes and was surprised to feel tears again flow. "Ever since we decided to stop our attacks — I've been thinking about my future."

"Alright," he said slowly, sensing the seriousness of her words. "So what do you want to do?"

She stopped walking.

"What's wrong?" he asked.

"I've put a lot of thought into this."

"Tell me," he said, stepping toward her.

She turned her gaze to the ground. "But promise me you won't laugh."

"Doina," he said softly.

She looked up at him anxiously. "I've been thinking that maybe —"

"You want to become a nun."

She smiled with surprise. "How did you know?"

"Why were you afraid to tell me about this?"

"I was nervous about what you'd think," she said, peering into the black sky.

He put his hands on his sister's shoulders. "I know how much you love the Church."

"It's so beautiful," she said, looking into his eyes. "And so different from this life we have now. I'm just tired of the killing."

"I know you are," he said. "And your burden is that you're so good at it."

She nodded. "That's why I want to dedicate the rest of my life to another form of insurgency. And my only weapon will be prayer."

Petre embraced her. "Just be happy, Doina."

"And it's alright that I won't have any children?"

Petre kissed his sister's forehead. "I'll take care of that for both of us. Elena and I will have a dozen of them. And I'll teach them everything we know."

"Good," she said.

"Except for one thing," he said, starting to smile. "You still have to teach my children hand-to-hand combat. They have to learn from the best."

She laughed through a sudden sob. "It's a deal." Doina broke from the embrace. "Alright, we carry out one more attack and then we start new lives." She dropped to her knees and swept leaves aside to make a clearing. "Final review of the operation."

"The target is a Secret Police safe house," Petre said, kneeling beside her and pressing his finger into a spot in the soil. "They're interrogating a prisoner they brought there yesterday. We've never hit this place before. They don't think we know about it."

Doina drew her finger in a line some distance from the point her brother had marked. "Here's the edge of the forest," she said.

"Got it."

"In Phase One, you shoot the two guards patrolling in front of the building while I rush out from the trees here."

"Understood," he said.

"In Phase Two, I burst into the safe house and take out the three agents inside."

"And we're sure there's only three?"

"Based on surveillance, yes. And they're only wearing side arms."

"You can handle them?" he asked.

"Last time I took out four. After my gun jammed, I used my staff to kill the one who kicked me."

"This from a future nun," he said with a smirk.

"In Phase Three, you run in after me. You assist with any clean-up and we make our escape with the prisoner."

"Plan confirmed," Petre said, coming to his feet. "Then we retreat back to our secret mountain to wait a few hours. Does your side hurt enough to be counted as a liability?"

"No. We have no liabilities." Doina got up from the ground. "Let's move."

They walked in silence through the forest for several more minutes until the lights of Brasov filled the horizon.

"It's time," he whispered.

They stood shoulder to shoulder in a custom passed down to them, repeating an ancient family prayer.

"We beg your forgiveness that we must take lives precious to you," they said together. "Have mercy on all the dead of our family and of those enemies we have slain. Grant them rest in a place of brightness and a place of repose. According to your will, O God, assist us in our efforts so that we can create a world in which peace profound reigns. In the name of the Father, and of the Son, and of the Holy Spirit," they concluded, each making the sign of the cross. "Amen."

They looked out from the forest at the outskirts of Brasov. Beyond the row of buildings visible a quarter-mile ahead, they saw medieval towers silhouetted by distant streetlights.

Through the sight of his rifle, Petre silently studied a particular single-story gray structure. It was the only building on the street that was illuminated from within.

"Two men standing guard, just like last night," he whispered.

"Good," she said. "Code names only from this point, Apollo. On one?"

"Doina, I —"

"Code names!"

"Diana," he said. "In case something goes wrong, just know that I love you."

She shut her eyes tightly and took a deep breath. "Nothing's going to go wrong."

He nodded. "On one, Diana." Petre crouched and focused his rifle sight alternately on the two men standing guard in front of the safe house.

Doina started the countdown to commence the operation. "Five," she whispered, "four, three, two, one." She bolted from the spot.

For their attack plan to work, Petre would need to shoot the guards the moment they noticed Doina. The sound of his shots would reach the building just before she burst in, preserving her element of surprise.

As he squinted to focus on his target, he saw Doina nearing the building. One of the guards turned his head and lifted his gun. Petre pulled the trigger and immediately shifted his aim to the cohort. The second man had not noticed that his partner was collapsing. Petre pulled the trigger again and scanned the scene through his sight. He spotted two bodies lying on the sidewalk just as his sister was kicking her way through the front door.

"God help her!" he shouted, jumping to his feet and starting his own race toward the safe house.

As he ran, he saw flashes of light through the windows of the house. He counted them and knew that more than one gun had been fired.

"Damn," he said under his breath, trying to increase his speed.

Petre reached the building and burst through the entrance. His eyes strained in the sudden brightness.

"You can relax now," Doina said softly.

He saw his sister standing in the middle of an empty room, five bodies scattered on the floor around her.

"You're alright?" he asked.

"Yes," she said, starting to smile. "We've done it, Petre."

"I'll feel better after we get out of here," he said, looking about.

"There were two more than we expected," Doina said sadly, looking down at the dead men. "God have mercy on them." She pointed to a man crouched in a corner. "There's our liberated prisoner."

Petre turned to see a man in a black robe looking back at him nervously.

"He's a Greek-Catholic priest," she said. "That's judging by the straight third bar on his crucifix."

"You'd know that stuff better than me," Petre said, kneeling down in front of the man. "Don't be offended,

Father. But we have to make sure you're not carrying a hidden weapon before we take you with us."

Petre ran his hands vigorously along the man's sides and legs. He looked up at his sister. "He's clean."

The man began to weep. "They did things to me," he whispered. "They did such horrible things."

"We know," Petre said, helping the man to his feet. "We're going to get you somewhere safe. But we need to move fast."

Chapter Two

Just before dawn, Doina and Petre stood at the top of a pine-covered mountain several miles north of Brasov. Their liberated prisoner sat on the ground a few feet away.

"We have to deliver him to another Haiduci cell," she said. "We're not equipped to get him out of the country."

"I know," Petre replied, looking up through the clearing above them. He could still see a single star directly overhead, but the faintest hint of orange light was spreading over the east. "All our old contacts are either dead or captured. Is there any group left that we can trust?"

"The Bear's cell, based at Red Mountain. That's about it."

"It's pretty far," he said. "If we left soon and did a forced march we could be there by midday. But why do you suppose they were interrogating a priest?"

Doina looked over at the man. "The Communists hate the Catholics just a little more than they hate us Orthodox," she said. "They know he has a boss in Rome, outside their control. Our own bishops have all but surrendered."

"Don't judge them, Doina," he said. "They have the survival of the Church on their shoulders."

"So do we."

Petre sighed and smiled. "I love this place. It calms me after all the chaos."

Doina stepped toward their guest and pulled a blindfold off his eyes. "How are you doing, Father?"

"Where are we?" the man asked.

"This is where we always wait for a few hours after our attacks. It's kind of a secret hideout. I hope you'll understand I couldn't let you see how we got here."

"And now I have another reason to love this place," Petre said. "Last week I brought Elena up here. Right on this spot we kissed for the first time."

Doina turned back to him quickly. "You didn't!" she whispered.

Petre looked at her in confusion. "She doesn't know what we do," he said. "Even if she did, she'd never betray us."

"Oh God, I hear noises," she stuttered, closing her eyes in concentration. "Someone's out there. Petre, we're surrounded."

"You're sure?"

"You know my senses."

"This is impossible," he said, his voice catching in his throat. "They must have found us some other way."

"That doesn't matter now," she said. "We need a battle plan."

"How about 'The Circuit'?"

Doina looked up in thought. "Maybe in full daylight. And the last time we used it we had our father's third gun."

14

Petre and Doina both instantly knew that there was only one possible escape route. A deep fissure ran down the eastern slope of the mountain. It was filled with pebbles and leaves accumulated over years. They had scouted it once as a possible emergency slide from the summit to the base of the mountain. They had also decided that someone could get injured in the attempt.

"We hoped it would never come to this," he said. "There's really no other choice?"

Doina shook her head. "Father," she said, grabbing the priest by his robe and lifting him to his feet. "You need to do everything we tell you or else we're all dead. Do you understand?"

"I do," he whispered.

Indistinct voices and sounds now ringed the mountain and approached rapidly.

Doina wrapped her arms around the priest and Petre. "Away we go," she said.

The three slid together down the naturally formed tunnel. Sounds of gunfire echoed around them as their attackers spotted the escape attempt.

For a full minute they tumbled downward, picking up speed as they went. A paved road at the base of the mountain suddenly stopped their descent.

"Status check," Petre groaned, rolling to all fours on the road. "How is everybody?"

"I'm alright," the priest said. "At least I think I am."

"I've got a problem here," Doina said quietly, holding her left arm with her right. She tried to get to her feet but then fell backwards.

Petre stood and walked slowly toward his sister. He saw her forearm pointing unnaturally away from the rest of the limb.

"Do what you have to do. Just do it quickly."

"My sister," he said, carefully taking her arm in both hands. "Relax now."

She shut her eyes. "Just do it!" she cried.

Petre saw her face turn ashen. "Take a deep breath, Doinitsa," he said.

Suddenly she opened her eyes wide. "Petre," she gasped. "Communism will fall."

"Of course it will." He moved her limb back into place, feeling and hearing the broken bones within.

"I'm sending you a present," she whispered, her eyes rolling back.

"You're delirious, Doina," he said softly. "Sleep for awhile."

"The Circuit," she mumbled, fainting away.

"I know. We should have tried it."

Petre sat down on the road next to his sister. "Get praying, Father," he said. "We're in some serious trouble."

***

Petre sipped some plum brandy from a small bottle.

"I'm ready for a bit of that myself," Doina said, taking it from his hand. She tasted it and shook her head. "Nope, not a good idea yet." She handed the bottle back. "How long was I out?"

"Just five minutes or so. That gave me enough time to get us away from the road and put a splint on your arm. What do you remember?"

"I remember showing you my arm and then I was waking up a few minutes ago."

"Before you passed out you said you're sending me a present," he said. "I hope you didn't give away a surprise party or something."

She chuckled. "I don't remember that." Doina held her arm carefully and stood up. "We have to get going now. They could be down off that mountain anytime."

Petre stood. "Now to the matter of this so-called prisoner," he said, turning toward the priest. "Maybe my girlfriend betrayed us. Or maybe you aren't who you say you are."

"What do you mean?" the man asked.

"Maybe you're not really a priest and somehow you helped them follow us," Doina said.

"But you searched me and found nothing."

"My brother searched you for weapons," Doina said. "For all we know you've got a transmitter in your stomach. Here's a test for you. Recite the Lord's Prayer in Greek. A Greek-Catholic priest would have learned this at seminary."

The man looked up at them seriously and got to his feet. "*Pater eemon, o en tees ouranees*," he recited. "*ayiastheeto to onoma ...*"

"Stop," Doina said. "You know, I still don't believe you. But we're going to have to take you with us for now. Don't think we aren't watching your every move."

The three started off through thick woods. The orange glow of morning flared to life on the horizon, coupled with a gathering fog.

Doina stopped walking. "Did you hear that?" she whispered.

"Yes," Petre answered in a low voice. "One person, somewhere behind us. I'd put him at twenty meters."

"No, there's two," she said. "One's twenty meters, with a second trailing him by another ten."

"Our liabilities are, obviously, your arm and this priest," he said. "Do you have a plan?"

"I don't like it, but we're going to have to split up. I continue walking with the priest. You stop and take up a sniper position. I'll fake the sounds of a third walker with my staff."

"Got it," he said. "I'll take them out one by one as they follow you."

"If I hear less than two shots, I'll throw some stones a few meters from your position to flush the last one out."

"It's a good plan," he said.

"On one," she said.

They continued walking and Doina began the countdown under her breath.

"Doina —"

"We don't have time to talk, Apollo," she said. "Three, two, one."

He turned and dropped to the ground. Sliding behind a tree, he aimed his rifle into the fog.

"Keep walking with me," Doina said to the man. "If anything happens, just fall to the ground and don't move, understood?"

"Yes."

Petre peered into an increasingly foggy dawn. His heart froze. Sounds were all around him now. Multiple enemies in every direction.

"*An ambush*," he thought. "*Must warn Doina.*" He fired his rifle twice quickly and then again after a slight pause. It was a pattern they had devised to signal the complete loss of a mission. He was instantly surrounded by men cocking and aiming their rifles at him.

A distance away, Doina heard the three shots and stopped in her tracks. She turned slowly to the priest. The man had taken a defensive stance.

"So you are one of them."

"I was just waiting for you two to get separated," he said. "Now drop that gun. I'm a trained fighter. I'll kill you if I have to, but I'd like to bring you in alive."

"How did you know the Lord's Prayer in Greek?" she asked.

"I *was* a priest. But then the Party enlightened me," he said. "Oh, and you were right about the transmitter in my stomach."

Doina took a few steps backward and looked at him sadly. "May God have mercy on you."

The man smiled. "Obviously it's not a fair fight with that gun. But consider yourself warned."

"I won't use my gun," Doina replied. "Take your best shot."

The man sneered and lunged forward. Doina dodged a swiftly thrown fist and swung her broken arm around. The sticks of her splint landed squarely in the man's throat. A crunch of broken cartilage rang through the forest. She gasped from the explosion of pain that followed.

The man dropped to his knees, grabbing his throat. He looked up in astonishment, trying to pull even one breath into his lungs.

Doina squeezed the splint with her good hand and felt the bones again find their proper placement. "My grandmother taught me that move," she whispered.

The man closed his eyes, still slowly clawing at his throat.

Doina turned around quickly and ran into the growing mist. "I'm coming, Apollo!"

***

Through the fog, Petre saw a flame sucked into a cigarette.

"Push that rifle aside, Apollo," a voice said. "If you help us finish off the Haiduci, you and your sister can go back to your village. We'll let you go free. How does that sound?"

Petre saw the glow of the cigarette flare up as the voice drew deeply from it.

"What will she do now?" the voice asked. "Your signal means that she's supposed to give you up for dead and escape to save herself, right? But she won't be able to do that. Without her beloved brother she's all alone in the world, am I right? So she'll try to save you. And then we'll kill you both. If you want your sister to live, push that rifle away like I said."

Petre drew a deep trembling breath. He tossed his weapon to the side. Immediately men snatched it away and pulled him to his feet.

Doina walked as silently as possible, hiding behind trees and peering into the distance. She could now hear dozens of people ahead of her.

"Forgive me, Apollo," she whispered. "I have to try something." She aimed her rifle into the fog. "*They'd hold you in the center of the group*," she thought. "*And so ...*" She turned her weapon slightly to the right and squeezed the trigger.

"Tell her to surrender," the voice repeated. "This is your last warning."

A man standing next to Petre gasped and began to fall. The next instant a gunshot echoed through the trees.

"She's good," the voice laughed. "But your time's up, Apollo. Tell Diana to surrender."

"Run away!" Petre screamed.

The voice stepped out of the fog and pointed a pistol. "Your choice." He fired a shot into Petre's chest. "Go get her!" he shouted to his comrades.

Doina shuddered at the sound of the single shot. Multiple guns now fired in her direction. She jumped behind a tree and heard bullets ricocheting off bark all around.

"I can't leave you here!" she screamed.

Another volley of shots rang out. She heard the sounds of approaching feet.

Petre dropped to his knees, blood spurting from his mouth. As he fell onto his back, he drew in one pained and gurgling breath. "Go!" he shouted.

Doina heard him. And she understood. She pushed herself from the tree and sprinted away. As she ran, she wept.

***

The midday sun had burned away the fog. Doina sat against a tree in a cool and now silent forest. She listened in every direction and knew that she was utterly alone. She buried her face in her hands and released a scream.

Doina grabbed the rifle beside her and threw it against a tree. "I love you, Petre," she managed through staggered breaths. Her face convulsed in deep grief. "And I didn't tell you that."

She stood and turned in the direction of the ambush. "What am I supposed to do now?" she whispered, tears flowing from swollen eyes. She picked up her rifle and hugged it. "Where do I go?"

Chapter Three

Petre awoke to a searing pain in his chest. He thrashed his arms and legs and found them shackled to a bed. Through blurred vision, he saw a large metal door set in a gray concrete wall at the other end of the small room. A single light bulb hung from a fixture in the ceiling and filled the space with a sickly light.

As his vision slowly cleared, the figure of a tall man appeared at his left. Petre squinted and made out the details of a thin black mustache and horn-rimmed glasses.

"I didn't expect you to live," the man said. "And I didn't really care. It was your sister we were after."

Petre recognized the voice from the ambush. "Where am I?" he groaned.

The man slowly took a pack of cigarettes from his shirt pocket. He removed one and lit it. "You're in Bucharest. Have you been here before?"

"No," Petre said weakly.

"I find it amazing how you rural types can spend your whole lives near a beautiful metropolis and never find your way there."

"I don't want anything to do with your Communist capital," he said.

"Ah, the fighter has returned. Do you have any idea what your life has now become? The doctors tell me to wait until you're fully recovered, but I say let's just get started."

He took a lengthy drag off his cigarette and extinguished it into his prisoner's arm.

Petre gritted his teeth and kept himself from releasing any sound.

"We've begun a little contest, you and I," the man said. "But no matter how long it takes, let me assure you I'll win in the end."

"You can kill me if you want. But you won't conquer me."

"Kill you?" The man lit another cigarette. "I know you're willing to die. In fact, before we're done you'll beg me to kill you."

He put out his cigarette in the same spot as the first. Petre closed his eyes and felt a wave of nausea roll over him.

"Not fun," the man said. "Not at all fun." He lit yet another cigarette. "Now let's talk about your sister. I forget. Were you awake when we brought her in here?"

Petre said nothing.

"We caught her crossing the border into Bulgaria. She said from there she wanted to get to Turkey and then the United States."

Petre turned slightly toward him.

"She didn't tell us all this right away, of course." He took a drag off his cigarette. "Let's just say that it took, among other things, quite a few of these."

He stood from his chair and leaned over to inflict more torture. Petre threw his arms to the full extent of the constraints, grazing the cigarette and knocking it to the floor.

"You're lying!" Petre shouted. "If you have her, then you go and get her right now."

The man nodded slowly, leaning over to pick up the still lit cigarette.

He took a drag and sat down in the chair beside the bed. "You're right, of course. But we'll find her eventually. No matter where she goes, we will find her and we will kill her."

He reached over and quickly forced the cigarette into Petre's cheek. Petre flinched and bit his lip.

"This is your life now, Petre," the man said. "And yes, I know your real name. When a brother and sister didn't show up for work at the collective for a few days, it was easy to figure out who you were. I have to say, that's quite a girlfriend you left behind. Let's just say that, before and after your arrest, she was more than cooperative with my men."

Petre pressed his lips together and did not respond.

The man lifted his cigarette over Petre's face. "Until you tell me everything I want to know, you can look forward to pain in every minute of every day."

"I know your type," Petre said sharply. "You actually enjoy this. You're just a weak man who's jealous of me."

"Jealous of what?" he asked. "You're a prisoner shackled to a hospital bed."

"You wish you were half the man I am," Petre continued. "But since you're not, you tie me up and torture me. You know that if I had one arm free, you couldn't even be in the same room with me."

"A bit of an exaggeration," he said.

Petre looked at him seriously. "No, it's not."

The man huffed and stood from his chair. He walked around the bed and then slowly unfastened the leather shackle around Petre's right wrist. He released the bond and took a quick step backward. Petre did not move.

Walking to the front of the bed, the man lit another cigarette.

"Don't you know that smoking is bad for your health?" Petre asked, smiling.

The man chuckled. "You have one hand free now, but I'm still here. Now tell me more about your operations against the Securitaté." He took a drag off his cigarette and leaned over slightly to put it out into Petre's foot.

Petre shot his body forward and twisted. In an instant, he had grabbed the man's index finger. He wrenched it sideways, snapping it at the knuckle. As Petre pulled on the broken digit, the man gasped and crawled forward on the bed. Petre threw the hand aside, and seized the man's throat.

His face grew purple as he helplessly clawed at Petre's arm. His glasses fell off and Petre stared into the man's wide and reddening eyes.

As the man thrashed his legs around, he upset a cart of medical instruments by the bed. The sound was still echoing in the room when two guards burst through the door and began pummeling Petre until he released his grip. One guard held the prisoner's arm down while the other refastened the restraint.

"I'll kill you for that," the man gasped, stumbling backward.

"It was worth it," Petre replied calmly.

"No," the man managed, still catching his breath. "I'll do worse than kill you." He turned and staggered out the door.

A few minutes later, a man wearing a white lab coat entered the room, pushing a cart of supplies. He was followed by a young guard in a gray uniform who carried a wooden baton. The guard held the baton against Petre's neck; he pushed his knee onto Petre's wrist. The white-coated man soaked a cotton ball from a bottle of alcohol and rubbed it on the prisoner's arm.

"Just don't move and you won't get hurt here," the medic said sharply.

Petre did not flinch as the man inserted a long needle into the main vein below his bicep. He connected an IV bag to the needle and hung it on a hook above Petre's head. Without looking at Petre again, he left the room.

The guard slowly released his baton and lifted his knee from Petre's wrist.

"Young man," Petre said. "You look at me."

The guard hesitantly raised his eyes to meet Petre's. "Is this Romania? Is this what you're fighting for?"

"I'm sorry this is happening to you," the guard said. "I'm just following orders. What do you expect me to do?"

"A revolution has to start somewhere," Petre said.

"Then I'll pray there's more people like you out there." The guard turned and walked out of the room.

As Petre shook his head, he felt a strange sensation attack his brain. It was like a severe inebriation combined with a succession of *non sequitur* thoughts.

"What is this?" Petre asked aloud. He gripped his jaw shut as another wave of nausea came over him.

The door opened and his torturer entered again.

"So you couldn't kill me," he said through a hoarse voice. "And now you'll be part of my experiments."

He sat in the chair beside the bed. "You're feeling a new combination of drugs. They've never all been tested together. I don't know what they'll do to you, Petre. But I'm sure they'll damage your brain. What do you think of that?"

Petre opened his mouth to speak against the man but heard himself talking about Doina wanting to be a nun.

The man laughed. "A nun? How pathetic."

As Petre closed his eyes, he felt tears flowing. He tried to whisper for Doina to forgive him but instead heard himself faintly speaking their prayer before going into battle.

"This is all gold to me, Petre," the man said, taking out a pad of paper and a pen. "Let it all out now."

***

By December of 1989, one by one, several countries of the Soviet bloc have fallen to popular uprisings. Anticipation builds that Romania could soon follow. On a small farm in Wisconsin, Doina has raised twin sons and trained them to fight in the coming revolution.

"One more exercise tonight," Doina said, handing pre-loaded clips to her sons. "It's time for a live-fire maneuver."

The twins stood at attention before her. Stefan and Andrew were identical, their tussled brown hair almost reaching their eyebrows, both dressed in blue jeans and matching olive-green canvas jackets. They were already quite tall for their fifteen years. Each had a staff in his right hand and a rifle over his left shoulder.

Andrew took the clip, unslung his weapon, and slapped it into place. "What's the mission, Mom?"

She turned first to the other twin. "Phase One. Stefan, you will sprint from here to the stream at the south side of the farm. On your way you'll pass the old wagon. I set it up in the middle of the clearing there."

Stefan huffed in frustration, and then winced for his mother's expected reaction.

"I have had more than enough out of you," she snapped. "Very soon we'll be doing this for real. The Poles, East Germans, and Hungarians have already freed their countries. When the Romanians rise up, we'll return to fight."

"We're only fifteen," Stefan stammered. "What good can we be against all those Communists?"

"Don't talk back to me while I'm describing a maneuver. Quick, where do Dimitrov Boulevard and Mihai Bravu cross?"

Stefan rolled his eyes. "City Sector Two. How about asking me something hard?"

"What's the name of the high school on that corner?"

Stefan looked down. "I don't remember."

"Twenty push-ups," she said.

As he dropped to the ground, his fingers sunk into the cold mud of a recently melted snowfall.

Andrew chuckled. "High School Number 15," he said. "I can't believe you didn't know that."

She turned to him. "What's the name of the library one block south from there?"

He opened his mouth to answer but then slowly closed it. "I ... forgot."

"Join your brother." She loaded her own rifle and aimed it into the distance. "Your uncle and I never even saw Bucharest," she said, squinting into the gun's sight. "But we won't bring down Ceausescu without taking the fight to the capital. And that means knowing every detail of the city before we arrive."

The twins finished their task and stood back up.

"Not another word from either of you until I'm done explaining your mission. Is that understood?"

They nodded silently.

"Good. Stefan, when you reach the stream you'll fire a signal shot to commence Phase Two. You then race back toward the wagon. Andrew, at that signal, you will sprint in his direction. You'll reach the wagon at the same time. On each of the four corners you will see pumpkins. Speaking in Russian, Stefan will signal for the attack to commence."

Stefan and Andrew caught each other's glance. Andrew smiled to reassure his brother, but got no response.

"Phase Three. Stefan, after you give the attack order, you will jump to your right," she said, switching from English to Romanian. "Using only throwing stones, knock the right-hand pumpkin off the wagon. Andrew, you will fire your rifle through the one on your right. You will each be employing weapons toward the other's position, but as long as you coordinate your movements, there's no danger of being caught in each other's fire. One mistake and someone could get hurt or killed."

The brothers again nodded silently.

"Phase Four. Andrew, after you've fired off two rounds, you will give the order, in Romanian, for the reversal. You will each somersault to your own left and attack the target again. This time, Andrew uses the stones and Stefan fires his rifle." She looked between the two brothers. "Any questions?"

"What's the name of this maneuver?" Andrew asked.

"It's called 'The Vice'," she said. "Your uncle and I used it dozens of times. It's very effective, but it doesn't forgive any errors."

"Then shouldn't we practice it with blanks first?" Stefan blurted.

She clenched her jaw. "Conduct the pre-attack sequence," she said, ignoring his question.

Andrew and Stefan inventoried their weapons.

"What are our liabilities?" Andrew asked instinctively.

"No liabilities," Stefan answered.

"We only recite the prayer before an actual attack," she said, a single tear running down her cheek. "Code names only from this point. Get going, Pollux."

Stefan took a step but then stopped, transfixed by the unexpected sight of his mother's emotion. The twins had never seen her cry before.

"Move it!" she barked.

Stefan headed toward the stream. Years of physical conditioning had given him a rapid pace. With the sun setting, the horizon showed forth a darkening hue of violet. In the growing blackness, Stefan felt an exhilaration from the speed he could achieve as he ran, jumping over every rock and root in a trail he knew perfectly.

He entered a thickly forested section of the path. Ducking under several low branches, he continued running.

"Perfect place for a trap," he thought, scanning each direction quickly. He spotted something pulled across the trail just ahead. With a sudden burst of speed, he jumped into the air, swinging his staff backwards to trip a wire as he sailed over it. Ropes snapped vainly into knots behind him.

Coming into the clearing, he caught sight of the wagon. As he sped past it, he noted the exact positions of the pumpkins his mother had set there. Stefan reached into his coat pocket as he ran. His hand rested upon a collection of throwing stones. Finding two of what he considered perfect shape, he pushed those to the bottom and pulled out the rest, letting them fall out as he continued racing.

Stefan reached the banks of the stream. After a moment to catch his breath, he looked up into the darkening sky. A crescent moon was just beginning to rise above the horizon. Filling his lungs deeply, he cocked his rifle and then fired one shot into the water.

Andrew had stood silently next to his mother, waiting for the signal. The echo of the shot reached their ears.

"Go, Castor!" she shouted.

"I know, Diana," he replied, starting from his spot.

Andrew sprinted, checking his rifle as he went. He could hear his mother's steps several yards off the path, keeping pace with his own.

Racing through the forest, Andrew scanned each direction as well, expecting to see signs of a snare. Spotting the ropes of the sprung trap, he leapt over them to avoid tripping.

"Good work, brother," he panted.

Andrew entered the clearing and saw the wagon. He pulled the rifle off his shoulder and dropped to one knee, taking aim and waiting for his brother's signal.

Stefan was also approaching the wagon, squinting in the near darkness to acquire his target. He jumped to his right and came to a stop twenty feet from the wagon. Withdrawing his first stone, Stefan hurled it forward. The thud of a successful impact sounded back at him, but he saw the target still tottering on the wagon. Quickly extracting the second stone, he threw it with yet more force than the first. The pumpkin exploded, the pieces flying off in every direction.

"Gotcha," he whispered.

Andrew's rifle was getting heavy from holding it in a constant aim. "Signal me, Pollux ..." he said in Russian. "What are you doing out there?"

Stefan realized he had forgotten to give the command.

"Attack!" he shouted. "Attack the target, Castor!"

The instant Andrew heard his brother, he fired a shot. But his aim had dropped slightly while he waited.

The bullet struck the wagon just under the pumpkin. He quickly re-aimed the rifle and pulled the trigger again, but found the weapon jammed. He panicked and moved the mission forward.

"Attack the target!" he bellowed in Romanian.

Stefan heard his brother and somersaulted to his left. He raised his rifle to fire.

Andrew was hyperventilating with confusion. "No," he whispered. "This is all wrong." He threw himself to the ground and heard the sharp whistle of his brother's shot pass just above his head.

"Code Red!" Doina called out. "Code Red!"

Stefan threw down his rifle and ran past the wagon. He dropped to his knees and put his hands on his brother's shoulders.

"Are you alright?" he pleaded.

Andrew nodded breathlessly.

"What's wrong with you two?!" she shouted, walking out of the darkness toward them. She swung her staff around, smashing Andrew's untouched pumpkin. "I trained you for better than this!"

"I screwed it up, Mom," Stefan said, turning to face her. "I ... I forgot to give the signal."

"You almost killed your brother."

"I'm so sorry," he said through trembling breath.

She leaned against the wagon and put her face in her hands.

The brothers slowly rose from the ground, looking helplessly at each other and her. She lowered her hands to reveal a tear-soaked face.

"It's my fault," she said quietly, looking up at her sons. "You weren't ready for this maneuver, but there's just no time left."

"You explained it fine," Stefan said. "It was my mistake."

She shook her head. "I know I've made your lives miserable," she said and threw her staff to the ground. "But I'm going to be leading you into battle soon."

"I'm scared, Mom," Stefan said. "I don't want to hurt anyone."

She smiled. "I'm glad to hear it. It shows I did something right."

"Are we really going to war?" Andrew whispered.

"Yes," she said, pulling both twins into an embrace. "But no matter what happens, don't ever forget that I love you." She squeezed them tightly. "When the moment comes, you'll both perform gloriously."

She released them. "Go back to the house. Get ready for dinner."

Doina stood alone in the forest clearing and looked up into the night. "Pray for us, Petre," she whispered. "This isn't how it was supposed to be."

Stefan flung the door of the farmhouse open with such force that it swung back to slam shut in front of his brother.

"Thanks a lot!" Andrew shouted, grabbing at the doorknob.

"What's going on here?" their father asked, coming from the living room. "How was training today?"

Andrew came through the door. "It was a disaster, Dad," he said. "My idiot brother can't follow simple attack plans."

"Stop it, both of you," he said. John Valquist still stood a foot taller than his sons and pulled their heads to his shoulders. "Settle down now. I've got a nice dinner ready for you boys. Your mother and I are going out for our anniversary and we'll have ice cream together when we get back."

He held them tight and kissed each of them on the top of the head. "I love you boys. Now go wash your hands."

The twins went up the stairs. Stefan muscled his way first through the door of the bathroom.

"For the record," he said, turning on the faucet. "Your mistake in Phase Four was at least as bad as mine."

"I know it," Andrew said, pushing his brother aside with his shoulder and wetting his hands. "Let's just be more careful when it's not pumpkins we're fighting."

Stefan scoffed. "You don't really believe in Mom's nonsense."

Andrew turned to his brother and flung water into his face. "Yes, I do."

Stefan shook his head. "The only good thing about this crazy training is that I throw stones so well that a baseball scholarship will get out of this stupid place."

***

John Valquist squinted from the high beams of an approaching car. "That's so rude," he mumbled.

Doina took his hand. "Thank you for a beautiful dinner," she said.

He smiled. "Phil from work told me about that place. It was nice." He cleared his throat. "How are the boys doing?" he asked.

"They're not ready," she said, staring out the window. "And we don't have time before they need —"

"Doina," he interrupted. "I wasn't asking about their fighting skills. How are they?"

"I'm sorry. I think I've pushed them too hard and too fast lately." She choked up. "And I think Stefan hates me."

"He doesn't hate you."

"I know he doesn't believe the stories about my family," she said, wiping her eyes. "Honestly, John, do you?"

"Yes. And I know you have to teach these things to our sons."

"Stefan's even better at the throwing stones than I was at his age. And Andrew, he's an incredible shot. I don't think I praise them enough."

"You'll have a good talk with them when we have ice cream tonight."

Her eyes gleamed with love and tears. "Yes."

He turned onto the winding road that would bring them home. "We celebrate sixteen years tonight, Doina. I cannot imagine my life if I hadn't met you."

She laughed. "I recall there was an army of Russian and Bulgarian women coming to that Church to land the handsome Norwegian convert."

"But then one day this Romanian woman walked up the aisle and kissed the icon."

"And what did you notice first?" she asked seriously.

"To be honest? Your legs."

"A dividend of all the physical conditioning," she said with a smile.

He kissed her hand. "I think that we were put on this planet for the sole purpose of creating those two young men. There's something great at work here."

She nodded. "You're right. They're a miracle."

He took a deep breath. "Do you really have to go over there, Doina?"

"It's what I was raised to do," she said. "It's what I trained them for. This is the moment of truth."

"Then I go with you," he said, looking in the rearview mirror at headlights approaching him rapidly. "This guy's going way too fast."

The car slammed into them. The angle of the impact spun their vehicle around. John and Doina watched breathlessly as they flew off the road and toward a large tree.

John opened eyes stinging from blood. Pain burned through his sides as he struggled to take a breath. He turned his head to look at Doina and felt a sickening crunch within his neck. He struggled through it and saw her; her bloodied head was slumped on her chest, a look of strange peace on her face.

"*Draga mea*," he whispered in Romanian. "My dear Doinitsa ..."

The car door opened beside him and cold air rushed in.

"John Valquist," a voice called out in slightly accented English. "Don't move. Is she gone?"

He turned his head back, feeling convulsions of pain surge through his body. John saw the silhouette of a tall man standing a few feet from the open car door. Behind the man stood a shorter figure. Both pointed pistols toward him. "Who ... are ... you?" John stammered.

"We were sent to finish something," the voice said. "I can see that she's dead. And you're not far behind her. Now we go to your house and kill those two boys of hers."

John closed his eyes and thought a simple prayer. "Please ... don't," he gasped. He felt a curious flutter within his heart.

A bright light flashed in the background, followed by a loud crack. The first man dropped to the ground.

The second figure stepped forward out of the darkness, showing John a face bathed in tears.

"You killed your friend?" John asked.

"I'm sorry I couldn't stop this sooner," the man said. "But I can't let your boys die tonight."

John drew in what he knew was his final breath. "Why?" he whispered.

"Because someone told me once," the man said, "that a revolution has to start somewhere."

***

Petre leaned against the cold concrete wall of his cell. Gray hair and a full beard spilled onto his chest above a tattered and dirtied shirt. He looked at a dim light creeping through the grated bars of the iron door. A shadow flickered outside.

"It's been a long time, Apollo," a hoarse voice said.

Petre strained in his mind to place the source. He coughed through lungs congested from the cold and damp air.

"Who are you?" he said weakly. "How do you know my ..." Petre paused, suddenly concerned about the security of his code name.

"I shot you that night in the forest," the voice said. "Do you remember that?"

Petre nodded. "I remember your voice."

"And what happened after that?"

Petre sat in confusion. A shadow and a ponderous doubt lay over the time between his memory of the forest and the cell in which he had spent twenty-seven years. "I don't know," he said.

"You still remember nothing else," the voice said. "That's interesting. Do you remember when we brought your sister in?"

"That's a lie!" Petre shouted, suddenly energized. "If you have her, then you bring her ..." He paused, feeling a sense of *déjà vu*.

"Of course, you're right, Petre," the voice said. "We didn't capture her. You always know when I'm not telling you the truth."

"What do you want from me?" Petre asked.

"You couldn't have learned it from this prison cell, Petre, but the world is changing fast," the voice said. "I had to take care of some unfinished business now. A few days ago, my agents killed your sister in the United States."

Petre felt the words as if a knife had gone into him and knew that they were spoken from truth. He dropped forward. "Doina —" he sobbed.

"Is dead," the voice said. "And I'm leaving you in here alive because that's the best way to punish you."

Petre's mind scrambled. "What did I ever do to you?!" he screamed.

A chuckle drifted through the grated prison door. "You still don't remember? How pathetic."

*On December 25, 1989, the dictator Ceausescu
and his wife are executed following a
revolution that spread through Romania and
culminated in the streets of Bucharest. The
orphans watch this news as it unfolds.*

Andrew and Stefan sat beside each other on the
couch of their aunt's house, listening to impossible
words streaming from the television.

"These are the first still shots the world has seen of
the dead dictator Nicolae Ceausescu," they heard.

The twins watched images of a man and a woman
lying next to a wall, death on their faces.

"In the last months, Poland, Czechoslovakia,
Hungary, and East Germany have peacefully
overthrown the Communist governments there.
Romania is the first to do so in a bloody revolution."

"Should they even be watching this?" their aunt
whispered to her husband, taking in the scene from
another room. "They've been through so much."

"This is history," he whispered back. "You know
what Romania meant to Doina."

She brought her hands to her mouth and caught a
sob. "My dear brother ..."

As she broke down, her husband put his arm
around her.

"I know," he said.

Andrew turned to Stefan. "I wish we'd been there," he said. "We should have been there."

Stefan scowled. "I don't want to talk about the training ever again, do you understand? It wasn't real."

Andrew leaned forward and put his chin in his hands. "I believe it was."

"And I don't!" Stefan snapped back. "So let that be the end of it."

Andrew tried to put his arm around his brother but Stefan pushed him away. They sat beside each other and continued watching the television.

Chapter Four

The Cold War ended. But others soon followed.
In the spring of 2004, Andrew Valquist has
been in one of them and soon will come home.

"I can't wait to see you," Stefan said, smiling through his words. His shoulder pressed a cell phone to his ear while he compared heads of lettuce. "When will you actually be out of there?" he asked, putting one of them into his cart.

"We fly out in three days," Andrew answered. "Then we spend a couple of days being debriefed and out-processed at our base in Qatar."

"What's that place like?"

Andrew laughed. "Camp As-Sayliyah is a resort compared to Mosul. I hear they have all you can eat 'Surf-n-Turf' in the Mess Hall. How are Kristie and John?"

"They're great," Stefan said, pushing his shopping cart down the condiment aisle. "They're sorry they won't be here when you arrive. They'd planned that trip to her mother's months ago. So we'll be batching it for a week when you get home. But don't worry, I'll wine and dine you in style."

"I can't wait. Listen, three guys are waiting behind me to use this phone. So I guess I'll see you in a week."

"I'll pick you up at the airport," Stefan said, turning toward the front of the store. "Be well."

He heard a click and looked quickly at the screen to confirm closure of the call. Stuffing the device into the pocket of his long black cassock, Father Stefan Valquist headed toward the checkout area. As he approached the store entrance, he noticed a sudden and strange silence in the normally bustling space.

"Hands up!" a voice bellowed.

Stefan's eyes quickly struck upon a masked man sweeping a gun through the area.

"Open that thing up," the man shouted at a teenage girl behind the cash register. "The rest of you take out your money and don't try anything stupid."

The half dozen shocked customers standing there responded slowly to the demand.

The man looked Stefan up and down while he stuffed money from the till into a bag. "What's with the black robe?" he asked. "You think you're some kind of ninja?"

"I'm an Orthodox priest," Stefan said, holding his hands up at shoulder level. "This is what we wear."

"I don't care if you're the Pope," the man barked. "I'll put a bullet through you all the same. Keep those hands where I can see them."

An elderly woman nearby began to convulse in sobs.

"You got a problem, lady?" the man asked, slamming the drawer shut and walking quickly toward her.

"Please don't …" she gasped, cringing from his approach.

Shooting a glance around his perimeter, Stefan spotted a display of canned vegetables within his grasp. Just outside his reach stood an assortment of brooms.

"You better shut up," the man yelled. "Or you'll be sorry real soon."

"Leave me alone!" she cried.

"That's enough," the man barked, swinging his gun toward her.

Stefan's hand snapped out to seize a can. An instant later, he had hurled the metal receptacle to smash into the man's face. The thief staggered backward in shock.

The priest bounded forward, his hand grabbing one of the brooms. He dropped to one knee and swung the stick forward. The sound of a hollow crack rang throughout the store as the wood exploded aside the man's head.

The astonished crowd watched as the thief collapsed silently. After a moment to register the unexpected event, they erupted into applause.

"You're a hero!" a young woman exclaimed, throwing her arms around him.

"Someone please call the police," Stefan said, gently extracting himself from the woman's embrace. He walked to stand over the man. "How is he?"

"Who cares?" the woman asked.

"I can't kill," Stefan whispered.

An older man knelt beside the unconscious robber. "He'll live," he said, looking up curiously. "But what do you mean you can't kill?"

"I just can't," he said, closing his eyes. "I'd lose my priesthood."

Stefan leaned against a wall, as the store became a chaos of sounds and motion in the aftermath of the incident.

The elderly woman approached him. "Thank you, young man," she said softly.

Stefan smiled faintly and nodded.

"Where did you learn those things?" she asked.

His eyes glistened. "My mother taught me."

***

"Who's the leader of this group?" Victor asked firmly. He stood in a small dusty room on the second story of an abandoned building which the SRI, the post-communism Romanian Intelligence Service, used as a safe house in Bucharest.

A single light fixture hanging from the ceiling barely illuminated the room. A stern wind howled outside the cracked windows.

The center of his attention was a middle-aged woman seated at a simple wooden table.

"Even the members don't know anything about the leader," she said. "But a very powerful man directs all our actions."

"This group you call SABIA, what is it planning to do exactly?" asked Dan, stepping out of the shadows into the range of the light.

Both men wore rumpled gray suits and sported crew-cut hair, the signature style of Romanian intelligence officers since Securitaté, Romania's equivalent to the KGB, held a reign of terror during communism.

She looked up at the men seriously, brushing dyed-red hair from her eyes. "The long term plan is the restoration of communist rule in Eastern Europe."

"How about short term plans?" Dan asked.

"Something big is about to happen," she said. "That's all I'll say for now."

"Why are you turning against SABIA?" asked Victor.

A smile of serenity came across her face as she paused in deep recollection. "I was at the Cathedral on a surveillance mission against the Patriarch. But as I looked at an icon of St. Andrew ..."

A long moment of silence passed, and then Victor prompted her. "What? What happened there?"

"I'm not certain even now. One second I was a secret Communist agent trying to gather information for our group. And then I just ... I just saw something in his eyes."

"Whose eyes?"

"St. Andrew's."

"What did you see?" Dan asked.

She smiled sadly. "I was reminded of a time when I was a little girl. I was at Church with my grandmother. The smell of the incense, the golden icons — I don't know how else to describe it. I just decided I had to make a change. SABIA gave me meaning once. But there has to be more to life than destruction. And I need to make up for the damage I've done." She looked up at them. "Does that make any sense?"

"What damage?" Victor motioned to his colleague to join him at the periphery of the room.

"As a SABIA agent I've been reporting on the movements of Church and government officials for the last twelve years. My work has helped SABIA prepare for the offensive."

"What kind of offensive?" Dan asked, joining his partner.

"Gentlemen, SABIA is about to unleash chaos in Romania. I can tell you much more, but I need assurances that I'll be protected. I won't continue this discussion until I know I'm safe." A tear ran down her cheek. "God forgive me for everything I did."

The two men stood together far enough away that she could not hear their whisperings.

"What do you make of this?" Victor asked. "Is she just crazy? She looks like she could be my grandmother. A secret Communist spy? Really?"

"It doesn't make any sense," Dan replied. "But when I told Headquarters that we had an asset claiming to belong to a group named SABIA, they insisted we take her here for questioning. I think they'd heard of SABIA before."

"All right," Victor said. "She certainly has a story to tell. So what's next?"

"We bring her in for a full deposition at HQ. If she's just deranged it'll be obvious under further interrogation." Dan took out a walkie-talkie and put it to his mouth. "Agent 45, bring the car to the back." He looked at his partner. "I'll escort the asset down to the vehicle and on to HQ. You stay here and transmit a provisional report of what she said."

"Sounds good."

Victor sat down at the table and jotted a few notes from the interview. He watched as his partner and the woman departed. The sounds of their footsteps creaked down the wooden staircase of the old building. Picking up his own walkie-talkie, he changed the frequency on the unit and pressed the button that engaged the encryption.

"HQ, come in. Agent 42 ready to report. Over."

"Go ahead, 42. Over," he heard in response, the words slightly distorted by the encryption.

"Agent 41 is escorting the source to HQ for further assessment. Subject stated that she's a member of a secret Communist group called SABIA. Over."

"Continue. Over," stated the response.

"She says that ..." He stopped as he heard a vague commotion one floor below. "One moment, please."

Shots rang out, followed by the thunderous noise of feet charging up the stairs.

He engaged his walkie-talkie again. "HQ, emergency here!" he shouted. "Repeat, emergency!"

The door burst open. Victor drew his weapon and raised it to face the intruder. Several flares of fire raced from the dark hallway. As bullets tore through his body, he labored to squeeze off even one shot, but collapsed unsuccessful to the floor. Looking up at the ceiling, Victor agonized to pull a breath of air into his lungs. Footsteps sounded at the doorway and walked slowly into the room, continuing in his direction. Through fading vision, he recognized a face above him.

"You!" he said weakly. "How could *you* be one of them?"

"One of them?" a voice said. "I'm their leader."

Victor raised his arm to make the sign of the cross. He was halfway through the motion when a bullet went through his brain.

Chapter Five

Andrew sat in the sparsely furnished lobby of his brigade's command center in Mosul, Iraq. Back in his quarters at camp he had finished packing for his redeployment to the United States. Then he had received an unexpected order to meet the brigade commander himself.

"The Colonel will see you now," said a lieutenant seated at a desk across from him. They were both dressed in the same light tan camouflage uniform, differing only by rank insignia.

"Yes, sir," he said, standing and walking hesitantly toward him.

"Right through that door," he said, pointing left.

"Thank you, sir," Andrew returned.

He opened the door, walked to the middle of the room, and snapped a salute to the man seated behind the desk. "Sergeant Andrew Valquist reporting as requested," he said crisply.

The senior officer, a man in his mid-fifties and nearly bald, stood up, still studying a sheet of paper he was holding. He looked up and returned the salute.

"At ease, Sergeant," he said, returning to his seat.

Andrew sat down in a chair before the desk, his stomach churning nervously about this unexpected meeting.

"Sergeant, I've been blessed with some excellent men and women under my command. But a few things caught my notice about you. I need some answers before you fly out of here later today."

"Yes, sir," Andrew said, feeling even more nervous.

"I've read a report on your squad. You saw a typical amount of action, but your casualty rates were lower than average."

"I also have been blessed with excellent soldiers under my command," Andrew said.

The Colonel nodded. "That doesn't explain everything. You made sergeant in almost record speed. You were awarded the Bronze Star three months ago. As you know, that's a really big deal. Your superior officers have told me that you perform like you've had Special Forces training, which, according to your records, you haven't."

The Colonel turned another page in the file. "They say you have a strange ability to detect danger. I also see here that you never studied Arabic formally. But a government linguist said you're better at it than her."

He closed the manila folder and looked up at Andrew seriously. "Who are you, Sergeant Valquist?"

"I'm a soldier, sir," Andrew said carefully. "I've always tried to make the most of all opportunities given to me. And I —"

"Cut the crap," the Colonel said. "If I had my way, I'd put a stop-loss on you personally and keep you right here. But even I don't have the authority to do that." He sighed. "What was your job before you joined the Army?"

"I was a Latin teacher, sir," Andrew said.

"A Latin teacher." The Colonel rolled his eyes. "I just want to make sense of this situation. You joined the Army in 2001, right after 9/11. You had regular basic training when you enlisted and you had the normal advance combat training before your unit was sent to Iraq. If you're somehow a complete fluke, I'll be able to sleep at night. Otherwise I'll always wonder if your talents could be replicated. Do you understand?"

"I do, sir. And there is a reason for the things you're noting."

"I'm looking forward to hearing it," the Colonel said. "So tell me how a Latin teacher from Wisconsin turned into such an exceptional soldier."

"It's pretty unbelievable." Andrew paused a moment and smiled distantly. "My mother was a staunch anti-communist from Romania who escaped from there in the early sixties. She raised me and my twin brother in the hopes that one day we'd go there and help overthrow the Communist government."

The Colonel laughed. "Alright, that's certainly an interesting start. And just what did she do that would equip you for that?"

"For starters, we were subjected to aggressive physical training," Andrew said.

"Did she herself have this kind of training back in Romania?"

"She told us that her father had trained her and her brother to take part in an underground anti-communist insurgency there."

"I've never heard of any anti-communist insurgencies, in Romania or anywhere in the Soviet Bloc. The United States would have supported such movements."

"She said that the Communists kept the insurgency out of the news even within Romania. Anyway, she taught us every aspect of warfare and strategy. As we got older, I excelled over my brother at the weapons, but he always had an edge in the hand-to-hand combat and the use of throwing stones."

"Throwing stones?" the Colonel asked.

"A family specialty handed down from our ancestors. As we got older, she also taught us Latin and Russian, in addition to her native Romanian."

"And why are you so good at Arabic?"

Andrew cringed. "Fact is, sir, I have a Ph.D. in Classical Languages and studied Arabic in college."

The Colonel raised an eyebrow. "Your file lists only undergrad. You purposely didn't let the Army know about your advanced degrees?"

"I didn't want to be turned into a linguist, sir. And I know that's what would have happened."

"The government could have used you in other ways. You may have committed fraud. This is a serious matter."

"I was told that underreporting facts is not the same thing as misreporting them."

The Colonel smiled. "Let's not split hairs on this. Anyway, it's over. Now, Valquist's not a Romanian name."

"No. Our mother married a Norwegian-American."

"What did he think of his sons being raised as little commandos?"

Andrew chuckled. "He loved our mother and believed in her plans. The training was a strange compartment of our lives. She would teach us this stuff for several hours and then we could finish the rest of the evening as a normal family sitting around watching television or doing our homework."

"So she must have been thrilled when communism ended in Romania," the Colonel said.

Andrew looked down in sadness. He reported to the Colonel the story of how and when his parents had been killed.

"And so you didn't take part in that Revolution," the Colonel said.

"No," Andrew replied. "To this day neither of us has even visited Romania. Our lives were pretty normal after that. We went to live with our father's sister. We graduated high school and went to college. My brother went on a baseball scholarship and even played Triple-A for two seasons."

"What's your brother doing now?"

"He quit baseball and went to seminary to become an Eastern Orthodox priest. He's assigned to a parish in Chicago."

"I'm a Catholic myself. You guys have married priests, right?"

"Yes. My brother and his wife have a young son."

"Your file lists you as single. Is that a lie too?"

"No, sir," Andrew chuckled. "Never been married."

"Why exactly did you join the Army?"

"After 9/11 I wanted to serve my country. And I'll admit I also wanted to see once and for all if the things our mother taught us were for real."

"Obviously they were."

"Tell that to my brother."

"You two don't get along?"

"No, sir, we get along fine. We just don't see eye-to-eye exactly on what our upbringing represented. My brother doesn't believe today that she was an anti-communist insurgent. He just thinks she was a bit crazy."

"And what do you think?"

"I wasn't sure myself until the first time I came under enemy fire here. But the training kicked in and I just acted."

"Based on your file, I would say your mother couldn't have been making it up."

Andrew nodded. "I know that now. My brother and I don't have to agree on it. I'm just looking forward to spending a lot of time with him once I get back."

"I see in your records that, upon your return, you will have completed your active duty obligations. So, you go back to teaching Latin now?"

"They don't have Latin anymore back at my old school. So, I'll need to start looking."

"You'll land on your feet somehow. Could I suggest that you send your resume to the NSA and this time include the transcript for the doctorate?"

"I appreciate the suggestion," Andrew said. "But that just feels a bit too much like the Secret Police my mother taught me to fight. I know they're not, but I'm taking things one day at a time when I get back. All I'm planning right now is to get roaring drunk with my twin."

The Colonel smiled faintly across the table at Andrew. "I've met a lot of interesting people during my years in the Army, Sergeant. But this is one story I'll hold this with me for a long time. Is there any chance there's a bunch of other secret commandos of Romanian extraction out there somewhere?"

Andrew laughed. "The only one I know is my twin brother. And as a priest he can't participate in combat."

The Colonel stood from his desk and formed a salute. Andrew stood and returned it.

"God bless you, Sergeant Valquist. You've served your country with distinction. Your mother would be very proud of you."

"I hope so," Andrew said. "Thank you."

Chapter Six

Petre stood before an icon of the *Theotokos*, Mary the Mother of God. In 19th Century Romanian style, it was painted on glass in a swirl of brilliant gold and green hues. He kissed it and crossed himself. As he walked back into the center of the sanctuary, the sound of his black cassock's flapping fabric filled the otherwise silent church. Despite spending hours in that place every day for the previous fifteen years, he never tired of it. Soft orange candlelight bathed the Church's walls, which were covered with other multi-colored icons against a sky-blue background. His nose sensed the hint of incense accumulated for two hundred years. Kneeling down on the floor, he whispered his prayers, closing his eyes tightly.

"*Doamne miluieşte*, Lord, have mercy, Christ, have mercy, Lord, have mercy on me a sinner."

As he leaned forward, chin to his chest, his flowing white beard tumbled to touch the floor of the Church. The long and equally white hair of his head was tied in a ponytail reaching the middle of his back.

Still murmuring his prayers, Petre did not hear a young monk creeping up behind him with a large open liturgical book. The youth suddenly slammed it shut, producing an echoing boom.

Petre jumped to his feet. "Doina, take cover!" he shouted.

The monk giggled toward the exit of the Church but found his way blocked by a tall and rail-thin man dressed in their same black robes. It was the Abbot, by title the 'Staretz', of the Monastery. From the look on his ninety-year old superior's face, the young monk knew he was in serious trouble.

"Brother Petre," the Staretz stated calmly. "Please wait for me outside. I want to talk with you for a moment, but first I need to speak with Brother Teofil."

Petre looked around nervously, still catching his breath from the shock. "Yes, Staretz," he said, obedient to his superior's request.

Petre walked past the younger monk, who looked to the floor to avoid catching his gaze. Passing out of the sanctuary, Petre sat down on the front step of the building.

"Brother Teofil," the Staretz said firmly. "You aren't the first person to play that prank on our Brother. But I refuse to let it become some coming-of-age rite for new monks. Who put you up to it?"

Teofil continued to look at the ground. "I am sorry, Staretz. It was Brother Daniel."

"I'll speak with him separately. What kind of punishment do you think is appropriate here?"

Brother Teofil looked up sadly. "You know best."

"Then you'll lose visitation rights for a month."

The young monk opened his mouth in surprise. "But my mother and father are coming up from Constanta this weekend."

"Tell them to cancel. Also, for the next four days, you will be Brother Petre's assistant in the dish room."

The monk looked back to the floor. "Could I lose visitation rights for two months instead?"

The old monk scowled. He knew that none of the monks enjoyed working in the hot and dirty dish room that serviced the monastery. Petre managed the large task alone most days. But the Staretz felt the punishment was fitting.

"No, you will assist him in clearing the tables and working under his supervision."

"Yes, Staretz."

"Stay here and pray to St. Parascheva on behalf of our Brother Petre."

"Yes, Staretz," he said, turning and getting on his knees.

The Staretz made the sign of the cross and walked out of the sanctuary. Coming behind Petre seated on the top step, he placed his hand on his brother monk's shoulder.

"Walk with me a bit," he said.

"Yes, Staretz," Petre replied, getting to his feet.

As they descended the stairs of the Church, Petre recalled the first time he had met the aged monk. When he had knocked loudly on the front gate of the Monastery fifteen years earlier, it was the Staretz, at the time just a simple priest, who had answered the door. Petre remembered the words of the Staretz on first seeing the newly released prisoner following the Revolution of 1989.

"You're the man from a dream I had recently," the Staretz had said. "Come in, but it will not be just for this night."

The two walked through an elaborately kept garden of flowers that lay between the community's white Church and a long red-brick building that served as their living and eating quarters.

"Who's Doina?" the Staretz asked.

Petre was silent as he contemplated a response. "She was my sister," he finally said.

"Was? She has passed away?"

"Yes."

The Staretz stopped and turned to him. "When did she die?"

Petre looked at the ground. "I learned of her death just before I came here."

"Why did you never tell me about her?" he asked. "Brother Petre, this is what I lament about your involvement in the monastery. We're supposed to be a family but you've spent the last fifteen years avoiding everyone and just living on the margins."

Petre nodded. "I try to do whatever work is needed. I actually like being in charge of the dish room. It's a job I think I do well."

"But you have a secret inner world that you have never let anyone else enter. Don't you think it's time to trust someone?"

Petre's eyes were misting. "I can't, Staretz," he whispered. "If you knew ..."

The Staretz smiled kindly. "Brother, I know you have something in your past. You told me years ago that you could never be ordained to the priesthood because of canonical impediment. That could be anything from adultery to taking human life. But I don't care what it is. I just want you to find some peace somehow."

"Not in this world, unfortunately."

They continued walking.

"I didn't actually come to the chapel to catch Brother Teofil playing that old prank on you."

"Don't be so hard on him, Staretz," Petre said. "As you know, they've been doing that to me for years. They see me as the crazy and confused old monk in the dish room. And they know what loud noises do to me."

The Staretz turned his head to look at him. "Loud noises startle you like they would a former soldier. Is that your background?"

"No," he said, believing that his strict interpretation of the question made his response not a lie.

"Brother Petre, I was coming to speak with you about something else. I've had a dream about you."

"What was this dream, Staretz? Your dreams have predicted the future so many times. Please tell me! What did you see?"

"First, Brother Petre, I don't predict the future. When I first came here myself as a young man of sixteen, the Staretz at the time identified the gift God has given me. It's not prophecy exactly. My dreams show me what will come to pass only in the realm of human action."

"But they're always so accurate. You've predicted so many disasters."

"Never natural disasters, Petre. Only those things which humans cause by their action or inaction."

"Why are your dreams always correct, then?"

"Because people are weak. They have no faith and they don't pray enough. Nothing I've ever seen really had to happen as I saw it. It could have been changed. A wise holy woman once told me that if only one person in every village in Romania had really been prayerful, the Communists would never have taken over."

They each crossed themselves, remembering the events of Romania's past.

"Staretz, please, what dream did you have about me?"

"It was strange. You were crying, but they were tears of joy. You were opening a present of some kind."

Petre raised one eyebrow and turned his head, thinking into the past.

The Staretz smiled. "This dream means something to you."

"It's ..." Petre closed his eyes. "It's like something I heard a long time ago."

***

SRI Agent Aurora Zamfir clenched her weapon in both hands and lifted it slowly toward a target ten meters down the firing range. It was to be a test of both accuracy and speed.

"Front sight on target," she mouthed silently. "Eyes on the prize. Smooth and steady."

A buzzer blared.

She squeezed the trigger and the gun discharged. The recoil on her Glock 9 millimeter service handgun automatically chambered the next shot.

Aurora lifted her finger until she felt the slight tap of the gun's hair trigger engage. From this point, the Glock allowed the rapid firing of shots within only a millimeter of trigger movement. She had another twelve seconds to fire off the remaining fourteen rounds in her clip. Any shot outside the small zone in the center of the circular target would drop her ranking from expert to merely marksman.

One ... she had touched the trigger to send the next shot ... she calculated mentally the three quarters of a second she could realign the gun before needing to fire shot number ... *two* ... "Front sight on target," ... *three* ... "front sight," ... *four* ... *five* ... she continued firing off the rounds, racing against the end of the test, *thirteen* ... *fourteen*. The buzzer sounded a split second later.

Aurora checked and double-checked her gun for unexpended rounds and then re-holstered. Removing her goggles and ear protection, she straightened her long blonde hair.

The firing range supervisor pulled the target off the mount and walked toward Aurora.

"Let's see how you did," he said, taking out a black marker. He crossed each hole on the sheet, counting the entry points. "Nice grouping here. Nothing even close to the edge of the center zone," he said with a large grin. "Very well done."

"All I know is what the SRI has taught me," she said. "As my first gun instructor told me, fundamentals are not basic. They're everything."

He wrote her score on the target and put it on a pile of others. "You've kept your expert status for another six months." He smiled faintly. "Want to attempt the other target again?"

Aurora raised her eyebrows. "Let's try it."

He walked down range to pin a new sheet on the mount. "Range clear," he said, returning to her position. "Prepare for the next test."

Aurora slapped a fresh clip in her gun and chambered a round. She removed the clip to top it off and put it back in her weapon. She now had fifteen shots at her disposal. Focusing down range, she saw the pattern of a human head and torso on the new target.

"This is unofficial," the range supervisor said. "Just do your best. Fifteen shots in rapid fire."

The buzzer sounded. Aurora fired all the shots with the same careful deliberation. When she had re-holstered the weapon, however, she saw a wide distribution of holes on the target.

The supervisor checked it over. "Only eight on the figure at all," he said. "But your position only requires you to be certified on the circular target. You've got a psychological block against firing on the human form. I've seen it before."

"I just wonder what would happen if I had to fire my weapon in the line of duty," she said.

"We could send you for special training in which you would fire simunition on actual people."

"Simunition?"

"Basically paint bullets from a gun with the exact weight and action of your Glock. A week of doing simulated maneuvers of shooting people would desensitize you to it nicely."

"But I don't have to do that, do I?"

"You're an Intelligence Analyst?"

"Yes."

"All you need is the basic certification you already have. Legally you're not even allowed to fire your gun except in self-defense. You'll retire from the Agency without ever using your weapon." He smiled. "Quit worrying about this stuff. I'll see you in six months for recertification."

"Thank you," she said.

Following a ten-minute walk through the SRI's palatial headquarters at the center of Bucharest, Aurora arrived back at her cubicle. She entered her password to unlock the screen on her desk computer. A long list of new emails awaited her. Most were the "Agency-Alls" she rarely read before deleting. One, however, caught her eye. She squinted at the sender and subject line and felt her heart skip a beat. It was a personal message seemingly sent from SRI Director Gheorghe Marinescu himself. She had never even seen the high official, let alone received an individual email from him.

"Impossible," she whispered.

She clicked on it to read a short message.

"Agent Zamfir, please come to my office immediately to discuss a new assignment."

She stood from her desk, noting the office number in his signature block. Taking out a small mirror, she gave herself a quick inspection and primped her long blonde hair. As she walked down the hall to an elevator, she adjusted her black business suit, pressing out creases and tucking in her white shirt.

Aurora proceeded to a top-tier administrative section of the building that she had never before entered. She spotted massive glass doors and knew they had to be the office of the director himself. As she neared them, they opened automatically. She nervously approached a receptionist seated behind a tall black marble desk.

"Are you Agent Zamfir?" the woman asked.

Aurora nodded.

"The director is expecting you. His is the only office down this hall," she said, pointing to her left.

"Thank you," Aurora said.

She walked quickly down the hall and entered the room through the already open door. Seated behind a large mahogany desk, she saw a tall man with short-cropped white hair, wearing a tailored blue pinstriped suit.

"Agent Zamfir," the director said. "Sit down."

He examined a number of files and then passed one of them across the desk. "Please read this report. It was forwarded to us a couple years ago by the Americans."

Aurora began to read:

//CLASSIFICATION: TOP SECRET - FBI NYC//
OCT 23, 2002
SUBJECT: "SABIA."
1) MIHAI LUCESCU, ARRESTED ON SUSPICION OF DRUG TRAFFICKING, INFORMED THE FBI THAT A GROUP NAMED SABIA WAS PLANNING TO RESTORE COMMUNIST CONTROL OVER ROMANIA.
2) SUBJECT STATED THAT SABIA [SWORD IN ROMANIAN] IS AN ACRONYM FOR "SECURITATEA A BATUT INIMICUL ACESTA" [ROUGHLY IN ENGLISH "THE SECURITY FORCES HAVE BEATEN THAT ENEMY"]. [NB: SECURITATÉ WAS THE NAME OF THE COMMUNIST-ERA SECRET POLICE.]

3) THIS SOURCE INDICATED A WILLINGNESS TO
OFFER MORE INFORMATION IN EXCHANGE FOR
LENIENCY BUT WAS FOUND HANGED IN HIS CELL
THE NEXT DAY, AN APPARENT SUICIDE.

Aurora set the report down on the desk. "This is
very interesting, sir," she said. "The acronym seems
kind of forced. I'll bet they picked the name SABIA and
only afterwards searched for what it stood for."

"Here's another report," he said, handing her a
folder. "My office compiled this from highly sensitive
information, as well as events of the past few days."

She continued her briefing:

//CLASSIFICATION: TOP SECRET — SRI — A10//
SUMMARY: SOURCES REPORT THAT FORMER
COMMUNIST ELEMENTS HAVE FORMED A GROUP
CONCERNED WITH DESTROYING THE NEW
DEMOCRATIC GOVERNMENT OF ROMANIA.
1) SOURCE REPORTS THAT A SENIOR ROMANIAN
SECURITATÉ OFFICIAL OF THE FORMER REGIME
CREATED A GROUP CHARGED WITH BRINGING
DOWN THE NEW DEMOCRATIC ROMANIA WHEN
THE OPTIMAL TIME FOR OPERATIONS HAD
ARRIVED.
2) THE SOURCE STATES THAT THE CURRENT
LEADER OF THIS GROUP IS WELL-KNOWN AND
HAS ACCESS TO SUBSTANTIAL FUNDS.

3) THE SOURCE INDICATES THAT THE GROUP HAS RECENTLY RECEIVED WORD THAT A MAJOR ATTACK EVENT IS IMMINENT. THE LEADER OF THE GROUP INTENDS TO GAIN POLITICAL POWER IN THE AFTERMATH OF THE ATTACK.
4) SOURCE IS NOT AVAILABLE FOR FURTHER INFORMATION AS HE HAS DISAPPEARED.
5) FOUR DAYS AGO (3/6) ANOTHER SOURCE INFORMED THE SRI THAT SHE WAS A MEMBER OF A GROUP SHE CALLED SABIA. (THE NAME SEEMS TO CORROBORATE AN EARLIER AMERICAN INTELLIGENCE REPORT.)
6) NO FURTHER INFORMATION WAS DERIVED FROM THE SOURCE BECAUSE SHE AND THREE INTELLIGENCE AGENTS WERE SHOT TO DEATH WHILE PROCESSING HER CLAIMS. THIS INFORMATION IS BEING PASSED TO ALL INTELLIGENCE COUNTERPARTS IN THE EUROPEAN UNION AND THE UNITED STATES IN THE HOPES THAT THEY MAY HAVE FURTHER PERTINENT INFORMATION TO PROVIDE.

She set the report down on top of the first and looked up at the director.

He sat back in his chair. "Agent Zamfir, someone inside this building tipped SABIA off to our safe house. Until the full extent of this infiltration is clear, there is no one I can trust. I've decided that the best way to approach this problem is to maintain a very small footprint. I'm asking you to accept appointment to the role of special investigator, answerable only to me, in the matter of SABIA."

A look of confusion came across her face. "Excuse me, sir?"

"Given the inherent danger in this appointment, I can't force you to do this," he added.

"I think you must have me confused with another agency employee," she said shaking her head. "I'm just an intelligence analyst, not a field agent."

"I looked at several people for this assignment. Let's see," he said, opening up another manila folder on his desk. "You're thirty years old. You graduated from the University of Bucharest eight years ago with a Master's Degree in Classical Languages. You applied to the agency originally as a linguist with French and Spanish capabilities."

"If you need an interpreter, I can certainly help. But I'm not someone to send on an actual mission."

He shuffled more papers within her file. "But then you cross trained into intelligence analysis because you wanted a challenge. That impresses me. And it convinces me that you have the ability to solve mysteries. Also, doing my own check of the duty logs, some of the more experienced agents had access to the information that was used to kill our men. And that means any one of them could be a mole. If I appoint a SABIA plant to this mission, Romania is finished. You, however, did not have access to any of it. You're clean and you can do this job."

"Can you please tell me what danger exactly is implied by this mission?" she asked.

The director leaned forward. "There are three agents dead just for stumbling on a SABIA asset. You would be going after this group both inside and possibly outside the building."

The image of the largely missed human target filled her mind. "Sir, I've never used my gun in the line of duty."

"I read in your file that you've consistently scored expert on your weapon."

"That's just at the gun range," she said. "How can I know what would happen in the real world?"

"Everyone has their first time," he said with mild frustration. "I'm in a difficult situation. There is a serious threat to our national security developing here. And I need someone inconspicuous to investigate it. But I'm not worried about you being able to perform under fire."

Aurora knew that this position could be a path to her ultimate ambitions of higher responsibility and authority in the agency. She had worked hard to gain recognition. She deserved this shot. At the same time, a part of her feared the danger.

Aurora swallowed hard and looked up. "I accept your decision, sir. I'll do my best."

As he stood from his chair, Aurora did the same.

"Your first priority is to find each and every person here at SRI who might be working with SABIA," he said. "You're to trust no one. By the time you get back to your desk you'll find you have total access and authority to prosecute this mission in whatever way unfolds for you. But do not stop just at the SRI. You are charged with investigating SABIA wherever that leads. Good luck, Agent Zamfir."

"Thank you," she said softly.

Chapter Seven

Andrew stood outside O'Hare International Airport in Chicago, Illinois, looking down the parade of arriving vehicles for the blue Buick his brother had described. He noticed people studying his tan camouflage uniform and assuming correctly where he had just been.

As a blue car pulled up, Andrew spotted a long black robe on the driver — confirmation that his brother had arrived.

Stefan stepped out of the car. "Damn, you look good!" he shouted, embracing Andrew tightly.

The brothers laughed as they looked at each other for the first time in thirteen months.

Andrew rubbed his hand in his brother's long beard. "You didn't have this when I saw you last," he said. "Kristie must really love you if you she lets you wear that thing."

Stefan shook his head, smiling at his brother. "To say I'm happy to have you back here ..." His voice caught in his throat.

"I know," Andrew said. "Listen, we're going to say all the things that need to be said when we're relaxing later. So let's get going."

Stefan and Andrew quickly threw several duffle bags in the trunk and drove away.

"What's our plan?" Andrew asked. "I need it to involve an excellent dinner and plenty of drinks."

"I propose we get you home," Stefan began, pulling out into traffic and peering at a mass of signs for the airport exit.

"And then?" Andrew said, adjusting the passenger seat to sit back. "I'm thirsty already."

"You shower up and get into clean clothes," Stefan said. "Then we'll go wherever you want."

"Really?" Andrew asked, testing the window lever. "I'll think over my options."

"Tell me everything that's happened since last we talked," Stefan said. "Was Qatar the vacation you hoped?"

Andrew began describing his travel up to that point while Stefan negotiated his way toward his parish. Every time they saw a building with the classic onion dome of an Orthodox church, Stefan identified the name and ethnic jurisdiction of that particular parish.

"Out with it," Andrew said during a lull in the conversation.

"Out with what?"

"You know you can never keep a secret from me. There's something big you want to talk about."

"There are actually two things. You know I believed that the whole Haiduci thing was a figment of Mom's imagination."

"That training got me through Iraq," Andrew said. "I had my doubts for a while too. But she could not have made it up."

"I'm starting to wonder myself," Stefan said.

He then described the incident at the grocery store to his brother.

"You didn't kill him, though?"

Stefan shook his head.

"I know the Canons of the Church don't allow a man to be a priest if he's taken human life." Andrew looked at his brother. "I never wanted to be a priest myself. And after Iraq, I never can be."

"I assumed as much."

"What's the second thing?"

"It's something I'm going to show you once we get home."

Andrew spotted a steeple in the distance.

"And this one you see on your right is St. Pantelimon Romanian Orthodox Church, also known as my current job."

Andrew looked at the grounds as they pulled up. A large modern glass building sat ringed with low shrubbery. A single thin steeple rose from its roof and displayed a large iron cross. Also on the property were two free standing red-brick buildings, which served as the parsonages of the senior priest and the associate.

"Ours is the smaller one on the left," Stefan said.

"If you don't mind ..." Andrew said hesitantly. "I'd like to go into the Church for just a moment first."

"No problem. I'll give you a quick tour."

"No," Andrew said. "I need to be alone for a bit."

Stefan nodded. "I understand," he said, getting out of the car. "Take your time."

Andrew went into the building and proceeded to the sanctuary, crossing himself three times as he entered. At the front of the darkened space he kissed the Icon of Jesus positioned to the right and then crossed the room to kiss an Icon of the Virgin Mary. Nearby he found a tray filled with sand sitting before a large crucifix — the traditional Orthodox shrine for the dead. Andrew took two brown beeswax candles from a small box and lit them on other candles already burning there.

"Mom and Dad, I miss you so much," he said, closing his eyes.

Andrew sat down in the front pew a few feet from the candles and looked up. Only then did he notice a massive circular icon of Jesus on the ceiling above him.

"Help me," he whispered. "I need a plan. Stefan's got his family, his ministry. What am I supposed to do with the rest of my life?"

Andrew sat a long while, listening to the silence of the room. He looked back at the two candles he had lit and smiled.

"I love you," he said. He stood up from the pew and crossed himself again. "God grant rest to my father and mother. May their memory be eternal."

Stepping backward from the display, he looked around the room. The icons painted on the walls were set against a bright blue background that he knew would be more vibrant when the lights were turned on.

He walked to the center of the room and faced the center altar, crossing himself again.

"I thank you for protecting me. I pray for all my friends lost there and commit them to your mercy and peace." He looked back up at the large ceiling icon. "And for the men whose lives I took. Grant them all rest in a place of brightness and a place of repose."

Andrew crossed himself three times and left the sanctuary.

During his time in the Church, it had grown dark outside. As he walked in the direction of Stefan's house, he saw the white glow of a full moon rising in the horizon. In that instant, he remembered seeing a full moon his first night in Iraq. He had told himself then that, if he survived his time there, he would see thirteen more Iraqi moons before he saw one in the United States.

"A place of brightness," he whispered.

Andrew approached his brother's house and saw the front door open.

"Hello," Stefan said, handing his twin a glass of wine at the door.

"If it's okay with you," Andrew said, "I'd just as soon we stay in tonight."

Stefan smiled sadly. "I already put two pizzas in the oven."

The brothers sat in the kitchen. They ate and drank and talked.

Andrew slowly set his empty glass on the table and refilled it from the second bottle they had opened. "I'm ready for your next big revelation," he said.

Stefan rose from the table and retrieved a folder from another room. "I got an email yesterday," he said, handing a sheet of paper to his brother.

"I don't understand," Andrew said. "Where the hell did you get this? It's a photo of Mom. But she's younger here than any picture we've ever seen."

"It was an attachment to a message," Stefan said. "The letter said, 'I'm a monk in Romania and I've tried to find my sister for years. If this is a photo of your mother, then I'm your Uncle Petre'."

"Mom said that the Communists killed him."

"I know," Stefan said. "I hit reply to this email and told him that the woman in the picture is our mother but that she's passed away. I told him about us and gave the number for the landline of this rectory. He's supposed to call sometime this evening to talk."

"Smart thinking, not giving your personal cell number, in case this is a communist plot," Andrew said.

They looked at each other and laughed.

"Oh my God," Stefan said. "Look at how well Mom trained us. We see everything as a potential conspiracy."

The phone rang. The brothers looked at each other.

"Let's see what this is all about," Andrew said.

"Hello," Stefan began, hitting the speaker function on the phone so his brother could hear as well. Stefan went into Romanian in response to the caller's language. "Yes, this is Stefan, and Andrew is with me. Listen, you can understand that we're a bit hesitant about this situation. It's not every day someone claims to be your long lost uncle."

"I want to see you two men," the voice said. "What can I say that will convince you that I'm your uncle?"

"One moment," Stefan said, turning to his brother. "Any ideas?" he whispered.

"Simple," Andrew replied. "The prayer."

Stefan smiled. "Tell us what you pray before you go into battle," he said toward the machine. "This is something only we, our mother, and our Uncle Petre would know."

They sat in silence and watched the phone. After a pause they heard a muffled noise, followed again by the voice.

"We beg your forgiveness that we must take lives precious to you. Have mercy on all the dead of our family and of those enemies we have slain."

Andrew and Stefan looked at each other, mouths agape.

"Grant them rest in a place of brightness and a place of repose," the voice continued. "According to your will, assist us in our efforts so we can create a world in which peace profound reigns. We ask this in the name of the Father, and of the Son, and of the Holy Spirit."

Andrew and Stefan instinctively crossed themselves and then sat in a stunned silence.

"Hello?" they heard.

Stefan spoke. "Uncle Petre, we need to see you. We're coming to Romania."

***

"Come to my office immediately," Aurora read in her email.

She stood from her desk and walked quickly the route she had taken for the first time two days earlier.

"Good morning, sir," she said, entering the director's office.

"Sit down," he returned, without looking up from a pile of papers he was studying.

They sat in silence for several minutes.

"I expected a report from you yesterday, which I never got," he said, still not leaving his desk papers.

Aurora swallowed. "I'm sorry, sir, but I thought you would only want to hear from me when I had something important to relate."

"What's the status of your investigation?" he asked, continuing to read his files. "Who's the mole?"

"I've studied the duty logs of everyone in this building," she started. "I believe I can narrow it down to three people who could have tipped SABIA off that we had a potential informant at that safe house."

The director raised his gaze from the papers. "And are those three people currently working in the building?"

"Well, yes, sir, and I —"

"You're telling me you know who the mole is but you haven't sealed the leak?"

"Sir, I don't have any evidence against them at the moment."

He banged his fist on the desk. "This isn't a court of law!" he shouted. "I put you in charge of stopping SABIA. Can you tell me positively that one of those three is the mole?"

She formed her words carefully. "With a great degree of confidence, yes, I believe that at least one of them was somehow involved."

"And are you comfortable that the mole is still working his job here and potentially passing on classified material to SABIA even as we speak?"

"No, sir, but —"

"Then cancel the clearances of those three agents!" the director shouted, leaning over his desk. "At least get that mole out of my building. Figure out who it is afterwards. I have given you total authority to act on whatever you find. Use it!"

Aurora stood from her chair. "I'm sorry, sir. I'll get on this immediately."

He looked at her seriously. "Agent Zamfir, are you afraid?"

"No, sir."

"Well, you should be. You don't think I'm afraid? You don't think SABIA would like to put a bullet through my head?"

"I suppose they would, sir," she said.

"And if they find out you're the lead investigator against them, they'd want you dead by the end of the day, don't you think?"

Aurora looked at the director. "I understand what you're getting at, sir."

"Perform your duty, Agent Zamfir," he said. "I expect daily reports, even if all you're reporting is that you haven't learned anything new. And the next time you come to my office, I need to hear something substantial."

"You will, sir," she said.

***

Aurora sat at her desk with eyes closed, breathing deeply. "Think," she whispered to herself. "You can do this."

She opened her eyes and bit her lower lip as she began opening programs on her computer. She prepared to cancel the security clearances of her three suspects, but then minimized that screen. Opening up the intra-agency email server, she began to type.

"What would a mole do?" she asked herself, composing a message. Aurora copied her creation into individual letters addressed to each of the three.

"I need to meet with you as soon as possible to discuss irregularities in your handling of classified material. Phone my office immediately."

She changed her signature block to describe her position as "Special Prosecutor, Internal Affairs" and sent the messages.

Her phone rang thirty seconds later.

"One of you has seen it," she said, picking up the receiver.

Aurora arranged a time to meet the first caller at a conference room a half hour later. As she spoke on the phone, she cancelled the clearances of all three, automatically blocking their access to anything classified within the SRI computers. Within ten more minutes, the other two had scheduled meetings as well.

***

"Who are you exactly?" Agent Mihai Bucur asked, sitting down at the table. He had left his gray suit coat at his cubicle, but otherwise he was a carbon copy of the other field agents in the building.

"I've just been appointed lead investigator into a computer leak that the techies found," Aurora replied. "We don't know the nature of the information passed or to whom, but your computer identification code appeared in the metadata."

"That's crazy," he said. "I haven't done anything wrong."

"There are a lot of explanations for how that might have happened," she said. "But you can understand that we need to investigate any potential security breach."

"Of course. What do you need from me?"

"First off, until this is resolved you won't have access to classified information."

"Yeah, I noticed that when I tried to keep doing my job after I called you."

"Secondly, Agent Bucur, you'll be relieved to learn that, in your particular case, I already know you aren't the leak. I'm just doing my job and need to do everything by the book until I can clear you. I'm authorizing you to take paid administrative leave for the rest of this week."

"Thanks," the man said. "Without access, I wouldn't be much use around here anyway."

"Don't worry about this," she said. "As I told you, I know you aren't involved. In fact, even at this early stage in my investigation, your file already records my belief that your data appeared in the leak erroneously." She pushed a file across the desk and pointed at a large font statement to that effect. "So, as you can see, there's really nothing for you to be concerned about. You're not under any suspicion. And this will in no way tarnish your record."

"Thanks," he said, standing from his chair. "I guess that does make me feel better."

"I look forward to calling you back to work soon," Aurora said. "There is a guard outside the room who will escort you to your desk to get any personal belongings you need and then see you out of the building."

As the man left, Aurora opened a file on the next candidate, knowing she would be giving the exact same speech and belief of innocence to all three.

"You're getting in way over your head here," she whispered to herself.

Chapter Eight

Andrew looked at travelers walking to their gates as he lifted a glass to his lips. "It feels like I was just here yesterday," he joked, sipping his beer.

Stefan chuckled. "Are you sure that you don't mind me staying in my full clerical clothes?" he asked, lifting the folds of black fabric on his lap in one hand while he held his drink in the other.

"Not at all," Andrew said, scanning the airport bar. "Besides, we're going to get steady traffic of attractive women who want to ask you things about God."

"Or tell me off in the name of opposing organized religion," Stefan said, sipping at his glass.

"Well, if they knew anything about Orthodoxy, they'd know it's not organized. I counted six competing ethnic jurisdictions on the way home yesterday."

"To his Holiness Bartholomew, Ecumenical Patriarch and Archbishop of Constantinople," Stefan said, lifting his glass.

"Bartholomew," Andrew returned, clinking glasses and then taking a drink. "And to his Holiness Teoctist, Patriarch of all Romania," he added.

"Teoctist," Stefan said, then taking a healthy swallow.

"What did Kristie say about this sudden trip of ours?" Andrew asked.

"She's not happy about it," Stefan replied. "She says the whole thing sounds strange."

"She's right," Andrew said. "But we have to do this."

"And she knows that. She just told me to be very cautious about this man."

"Good advice regardless," Andrew noted.

They each saw a young woman looking at them from a distance.

"Here's our first customer," Andrew whispered, as the woman hesitantly approached their table.

"Hello," Stefan offered as she stopped in front of them. "Can we help you, miss?"

"Excuse me, Father," she said. "I can't tell you how happy I am that I found a Catholic priest here at the airport."

"First of all," Stefan said, "I'm not Catholic."

"Really? What are you?"

"I'm Eastern Orthodox."

"What's that?"

"We're very close to the Catholics, but not identical," Andrew said.

"But you are a priest?" she asked Stefan.

"I am."

"Good. I have this cross I wear," she said, producing a small gold necklace from within her blouse and removing it. "But it's been a long time since I went to Church and I never got around to having it blessed. I guess I would feel better getting on a plane if I took care of that."

"I understand," Stefan said. He reached into his carry-on bag to produce a little bottle.

"Hold your cross like so," he told her, positioning her hand in front of him. "This is Holy Water," he explained, pouring a few drops of it onto the cross. "Like your own priests, there's a much fuller ritual I would use if I was at my Church, but a short prayer will be sufficient."

"Excellent," she said.

"Almighty God, bless this cross," he continued. "May it remind us of your sacrifice for sin and be an emblem of protection against all attacks of the enemy. In the name of the Father, and of the Son, and of the Holy Spirit." Stefan made the sign of the cross over her hand.

"Is that it?" she asked.

"Yes. Have a nice flight and God bless you," Stefan added.

"Thanks," she said.

They watched her take a few steps away and then turn back toward them slowly.

"Excuse me," she said. "But is an Orthodox blessing ... um ... ?"

Stefan grinned. "It's valid. In fact, the Roman Catholic Church considers my ordination and all the sacraments I perform to be valid."

"Good," she said, nodding. "I won't bother you anymore."

"It's no problem, miss," he said. "One more thing, though. You've reached out to God in advance of this trip. And that's good. Reach out to him again soon."

She looked at him seriously. "I will, Father." She walked away.

The twins each took drinks off their beers.

"That was very pleasant," Andrew finally said. "But you could have positioned her just a bit more to my left. Let's just say it would have given me an even more interesting silhouette."

Stefan rolled his eyes. "How could you possibly sexualize that spiritual moment?"

Andrew finished his drink. "Are you kidding me? Touching hands, drops of water?" He motioned for the bartender to refill their drinks. When they were restocked, he raised his glass. "It was a strange enough encounter, a lovely Catholic woman trying to get a blessing from an Orthodox priest in an airport bar."

"It'll probably be the first of a dozen curious things on our little vacation together," Stefan said. "We'll keep a running list."

"Agreed." Andrew raised his glass. "To his Holiness John Paul the Second, Bishop of Rome?" he asked hesitantly.

"Of course," Stefan said, clinking their glasses.

***

With the sunlight nearly faded, Aurora pulled into the dark garage of her apartment building.

"*This is where I would do it*," she thought to herself. "*Since he believes he's not a suspect, he'll think*

96

he can get away with it." She checked her gun and put it back in her shoulder harness. *"Someone will try to kill me when I get out of this car."*

Scanning the empty garage, she looked for any signs of a hidden assailant. Her fingers were trembling as she lifted her hand to open the door.

"Front sight," she whispered. "Eyes on the prize."

Aurora left her car and began walking toward the elevator at a normal pace. Another car door opened nearby. She tried hard to seem casual as she turned around. A tall young man stepped out of a vehicle behind her.

"Excuse me, miss," he said. "My car needs a jump. Can you help me out?"

Aurora drew her gun. "Hands up!" she shouted.

"Hey, hold on," the man said, putting his hands forward. "Settle down. I just wanted your help, is all."

"I know what you're here for," she said. "Hands up immediately or I'll shoot. Do you understand?"

The man slowly put his hands up. "How about I just get back in my car and get out of here, okay?"

"I thought you needed a jump?"

Aurora saw his arms move downward. In an instant, he had pulled a pistol from his jacket and was lifting it toward her. She squeezed the trigger and saw sparks jumping off the wall behind the man. A massive blow struck her chest. She fought to reposition her gun and fired off another shot. The man collapsed to the ground.

As the echoes of gunshots subsided, Aurora saw a black hole on the man's forehead, a stream of blood oozing out. With trembling hands, she took out her walkie-talkie and fell to her knees.

"Agent down," she managed, struggling to catch her breath. "I need immediate assistance."

***

"That's quite a stupid stunt you pulled yesterday," the director said. "How do you feel?"

"My ribs still hurt quite a bit," Aurora answered. "But I'm ready to be back on the job."

"Good. So explain why you thought facing SABIA in single combat was a good idea."

Aurora looked at him seriously. "I did what you told me to do, sir. I'm taking full control of this investigation and so I pursued an action I felt would flush someone out."

"By using yourself as a decoy? You know, there are plenty of ways to get killed while wearing a bulletproof vest. He could have had armor piercing bullets. Or he could have gotten a shot off into your head."

"That's how I killed him."

"I've read the report on the scene," the director said. "Your hit ratio was awful."

"It won't be next time, sir," she said.

He smiled. "I believe that. So tell me what we've learned."

"I assumed our mole wasn't going to do the hit himself," she began. "He believes he's officially not under suspicion at this time. But neither could he let me continue digging around. So they sent a SABIA member with no connection to the SRI for this hit."

"What do we know about the assassin?"

"Not surprisingly, he had no identification on him. Just a single cell phone that we're examining. Hopefully something will connect him to one of the three men I suspect."

The director leaned over his desk. "And what makes you think they won't try another hit on you?"

"They will, sir," she said. "And that's why I've checked out one of the guest rooms in the building until this case is resolved."

"Did I approve that?"

"You didn't have to. I did."

He laughed. "Good work, Agent Zamfir. Keep me informed of all developments."

***

The brothers walked up the ramp from their airplane.

"Get ready to actually enter Romania," Stefan said, as they reached a set of large glass doors.

The moment they entered the airport terminal, their eyes fell on a large illuminated advertisement of a beautiful young woman with blaze red hair, wearing a short, low cut, emerald green dress.

"If this is Romania," Andrew said, "then I approve."

Stefan laughed. "That's Vali, the hottest Romanian diva at the moment."

"I can't imagine one hotter. But how are you so up on Romanian Pop Culture?"

"The kids at my parish rave about her. So I got her latest album to see what the fuss was all about."

Andrew approached the ad and examined it. "She's remarkably fit. It says she's giving a concert here in Bucharest in a few days." He turned to his brother and smiled. "I say we should be in attendance."

"We came to spend time with our long lost uncle," Stefan said. "Do you suppose he'd like to see her?"

Andrew put his hand to his chest. "She's stunning. I'm afraid that any encounter with such a perfect specimen would probably be the death of an elderly monk."

"Some other time then," Stefan said, pulling his brother along.

They proceeded through passport control and rode people mover conveyer belts down a long corridor to the baggage area. Three more ads featuring Vali in increasingly provocative poses met them on the way.

"This is torture!" Andrew exclaimed. "I must see that concert."

"Why did we never visit Romania before?" Stefan asked, changing the subject.

"It's hard to plan a vacation in a country you once plotted and trained to overthrow," Andrew replied.

They arrived in the spacious baggage claim area. A sky roof brilliantly illuminated the space.

Andrew took one of their suitcases off the conveyer belt. "Our childhood really was a casualty of the Cold War," he said. "Even now my mind is recalling the terrain surrounding this airport to plan escape routes in the event of an ambush."

A young brunette woman in a long red dress came and stood next to them. She alternated between looking at her watch and the passing luggage.

"Excuse me," Andrew said to her. "Do you speak English?"

"Yes, I do," she said with a moderately strong accent.

"I'm here on vacation," he started. "But I've been trying to learn Romanian for the trip. Can I try to practice with you a bit?"

"*Sigur că da,*" she said, smiling. "Of course."

Andrew looked up as if searching for words. "I'm pleased to be here in this Romania," he said, putting an American accent and some errors into his speaking. "You're beautiful woman to help me for learning this."

Stefan rolled his eyes.

She smiled and put her hand on his shoulder. "You speak Romanian very well."

"I'm sorry, I not to understand. More slow, please?" he said.

"You speak very well," she said slowly, leaning toward him. "How long have you been learning?"

"In two month ago I start," Andrew said. "Tonight you plan here in Romania?"

"My American cousin is just here for a visit," Stefan said in perfect Romanian. "He's a monk in the United States, but he wanted to see all the beautiful monasteries in this country."

"Oh, I understand," she said, removing her hand and stepping back. "Enjoy your time here." She spotted her bag and left quickly.

"Thanks a lot!" Andrew said. "I think I could've gotten a lot of mileage out of the 'American who learned just a little Romanian' bit."

"I'll make you a monk every time, just to warn you. But don't you think that an American combat veteran who happens to speak natively fluent Romanian would be even more interesting?"

"Huh," Andrew said. "You might be on to something there. Add in the fact that my twin brother is a priest and I'm just exactly the guy a Romanian woman would want to take home to mother."

Stefan turned around, taking in the scene of the fully modern terminal, polished marble floors and glowing advertisements. "Look at this place. It's hard to believe this was a dismal Communist country just fifteen years ago. Apart from all the signs being in Romanian, this airport could be anywhere in the world."

Andrew took their last bag off the conveyer belt. "What's our plan from here?" he asked.

"I always prefer adventures in public transportation," Stefan said. "But let's indulge ourselves in a nice taxi to the hotel."

"Agreed. Tomorrow morning when we go to the Monastery we'll see things closer up."

The brothers walked past the customs area and entered a large hall teeming with people holding up signs for arriving business guests. Leaving the terminal, they approached a taxi by the curb.

"Good afternoon, Father," the taxi driver said in English. "Where can I take you?"

Stefan leaned in the passenger side window. "How much to the Majestic?" he asked in Romanian.

"Fifty American dollars," the driver responded, still in English.

"How do you know I'm American?" Stefan said.

"Your shoes."

"Forty, and ten more for a tip," Stefan said, grinning.

"Agreed."

They left the airport area and immediately entered stop-and-go traffic creeping into the city itself. Newly built glass office buildings appeared sporadically among endless series of gray concrete apartment blocks constructed during the communist period.

As their taxi crawled toward the city center, Andrew and Stefan showed each other landmarks they had previously known only from their mother's constant instruction.

"Could Ana Ipătescu Boulevard be a way around this traffic?" Andrew asked their driver.

The man laughed loudly. "I haven't heard it called that for years!"

"Did they change the name?" Stefan asked. "What is it now?"

"Well, it used to be Colței Boulevard. Then the Communists changed it to Ana Ipătescu. Since the Revolution, it's Lascăr Catargiu."

Andrew chuckled. "In other words, our mother grilled us for hours at a time on street names that are all gone now," he whispered to Stefan.

"Now I'm glad I never learned communist era Bucharest as well as you."

Chapter Nine

"I'm unpacked," Stefan said, sitting down on his bed in the hotel room. "Let's get cleaned up and then go out and find some food."

"Sounds good," Andrew said, flipping through the channels on the television. "Shouldn't we first confirm tomorrow's plans with Uncle Petre?"

"Good idea," Stefan replied, digging through his wallet for the number. "Do you suppose Petre has some authority in this monastery?"

"Why would you think that?"

"I just can't imagine that every monk has his own cell phone."

Andrew raised one eyebrow. "We'll see tomorrow, I guess."

He continued flipping through the local programs while he heard Stefan discuss their arrival and plans to meet at the monastery the following morning.

"Ask him what the best public transportation would be," Andrew added. "Since all the street names have changed, I'm feeling lost in this city."

Stefan concluded the call. "He said there's a Metro stop at the Piața Universității. From there we have one transfer and then it's a short walk from what he called Piața Obor."

"We'll still look it over on a map. Listen, I'm starving. Let's take showers and go find a nice restaurant."

"I'll go first," Stefan said. "Maybe you can call the front desk and get a nice recommendation. There's got to be something in this area within walking distance."

"Will do," Andrew said.

Andrew waited until he heard the water of the shower turn on and then picked up the phone.

"Hello, front desk? I just checked into room 210. You're Anela, right?" Andrew smiled and turned off the television. "I need some information but I was also hoping I could practice my Romanian a bit with you. Great, I'll be right down."

***

"Anything further from the assassin's cell phone?" the director asked.

"No, sir," Aurora said, leaning back in her accustomed chair in his office. "I can't link him up with any of the three agents I suspended. And I still can't pin anything on those men except that I know one of them has to be the SABIA mole."

"All three of your suspects are Level 4 covert specialists. They're so good that I wouldn't expect them to leave a trace of evidence behind."

"I'm still looking at the data from a number of different angles," Aurora said. "Something may yet stand out."

"You have them under surveillance, right?"

"Of course," she said. "But all three have proven their ability to lose their tails every time they leave their homes."

The director chuckled. "Again, we've trained them very well. But unless we actually charge them with something, we can't do more than just try to follow them and conduct more research."

Aurora shook her head. "You didn't have these problems when you were a junior officer in the Securitaté before the Revolution, did you?"

The moment the words left her mouth, she wished she could have pulled them back. She braced herself for his response.

The director nodded slowly. "Obviously, under communism we would have tortured all three and probably all three would have confessed. But we would have also discovered the truth eventually." He looked at her seriously. "I was following orders just like all the rest. That doesn't make it right, but that's what it was. After the Revolution, the fact is that the provisional government had no choice but to grandfather a bunch of us into the new intelligence agencies. After all, we were the only ones around who knew how to be spies. But I swore allegiance to the newly democratic government with a serious sincerity of heart, Agent Zamfir."

"I wasn't suggesting otherwise, sir," she said quickly.

"Let me ask you something," he started. "Do you wish you had more powers to conduct this investigation?"

"It's the classic tension between liberty and security. Sir, I don't personally believe in God. But I love the fact that Romania's churches are filled every Sunday with people free to worship as they choose. Our liberated Romania is a better place to live than the safe but cowering state my parents served."

He smiled. "That's the right answer, Agent Zamfir." He looked at his desk. "I may have a new lead for you," he said, picking up one of the sheets.

"Excellent," she replied. "I'll chase it down. What do you have exactly?"

"Tell me first what you know about the Haiduci."

"The Haiduci?"

"Anything?"

Aurora looked at the ceiling, trying to remember the substance of only one report she had read.

"They were an anti-communist insurgency that was active in Romania mainly north of Bucharest from 1949 down to 1962. After that they were finally eradicated."

"Nice dictionary definition," he said. "And if you went into the streets of Brasov today and asked people about it, what would you hear?"

"Almost nothing, sir," Aurora answered. "The Communists conducted an aggressive misinformation campaign. Most of the country still doesn't know it even happened."

"Right," he stated. "Now to the more pertinent question. What do you suppose SABIA would think of the Haiduci? Or what would the Haiduci think of SABIA?"

Aurora considered the matter. "Well, I suppose they'd be mortal enemies. But why does this matter? SABIA is a problem right now. The Haiduci are long gone."

"Indeed they are," he said. "But then something rather strange happened today. The old Securitaté kept tabs on a few Haiduci who managed to escape Romania after their insurgency was finally blotted out. Even after the Revolution, information about them stayed in databases of the intelligence agencies. This caused a report to be automatically generated this morning by a Transportation Agency computer. It seems the twin sons of one of the greatest Haiduci fighters that ever lived landed here in Bucharest a few hours ago." He pushed a piece of paper across the desk.

Aurora looked at the brief report. "Have they ever visited Romania before?" she asked.

"No, and I have a hard time believing this could be a coincidence."

"Is this mine?" she asked, waving the sheet.

"Yes."

She put the paper in her briefcase. "If it's not a coincidence, what could this mean?"

"Your guess is as good as mine. One thing we don't need is a couple of Americans getting hurt in Romania. From a tourism standpoint, that shouldn't happen."

"I think I need to see for myself what they're up to," she said.

"How will you do that?"

Aurora smiled. "First I find them. I'll keep you posted on anything I learn about this issue." She stood from her chair. "Sir, I have one more matter I would like to bring up before trying to meet our American visitors."

He nodded.

"If there really is an imminent attack here in Romania, we need to look at the appropriateness of large public gatherings."

He rubbed his eyes. "This is what I hate about tenuous threat intelligence. It's easy to overreact, but if you do nothing you're in trouble afterwards. What do you have in mind?"

"There are two events that I think should be cancelled until we can find out more about this threat. There is an ordination of a number of priests at the Cathedral tonight and, of course, the Vali concert on Sunday."

"Sorry to say, even I don't have the authority to cancel things like that."

"Can we at least order the local authorities to increase security?" she asked.

"What do you propose?"

"I would like all attendees to go through metal detectors," she said.

"Sounds reasonable," he said. "I'll discuss it with the other agencies. You've really suddenly grown into this position, Agent Zamfir," the director said. "I'm feeling good about choosing you."

"Thank you, sir," she replied. "And if you'll excuse me, I'm going to go talk to the Haiduci."

Chapter Ten

"Table for two, non-smoking, please," Stefan said to the concierge.

"Right this way, Father," the man said.

They followed him to a booth on the far side of the dining room. The room was softly lit from crystal chandeliers, with velvet maroon and gold-laced wallpaper embracing the space.

Andrew stepped ahead of his brother to take the seat facing out onto the other diners.

"I hope you'll understand that this spot would be kind of lost on you," he said.

Stefan smiled with understanding. "Just because I'm married you don't think I can appreciate feminine beauty?" he asked. "Alright, you can have that seat, but that means I get control of the television for the rest of the trip."

Andrew winced and thought it over. "Granted," he said.

A moment later a young waitress appeared, wearing an embroidered white peasant blouse.

"What can I start you gentlemen off with?" she asked in English, handing them menus.

"Do we have a neon sign above us flashing 'Americans'?" Andrew asked in Romanian.

The waitress laughed. "Asking for non-smoking is the first hint."

"A carafe of the house red wine," Stefan replied with a grin.

"Right away," she said, and turned around quickly.

Andrew leaned into the air swirled by her brown ponytail and slowly breathed in the scent of her perfume.

"Oh my God," Stefan said. "You're really a mess! I thought your conduct was just normal guy-on-vacation banter. But you've got something way off kilter in your hormones, don't you?"

Andrew nodded. "Don't think I don't know it. My last serious relationship ended when Janet found out I was going to Iraq."

"Oh, I remember that one," he said. "Opposed to the war on philosophical grounds and she didn't have the energy to explain why her boyfriend was over there fighting."

"But she was hot," Andrew said.

The waitress returned and filled large glasses with wine, setting the rest of the carafe between them.

"Thank you so much," Andrew responded, smiling broadly.

She giggled and departed.

"*Noroc*," Andrew said. "Cheers."

They drank deeply and set their glasses down.

"Fact is," Andrew continued, "there's something about being in a place where you might get killed at any second which just charges you emotionally. I've heard people say that the experience just amplifies who you really are."

"And you've always had a weakness for women," Stefan said.

"Right. So now I find myself lost in the eyes and hair and smells and curves of virtually every woman we see."

"Wow," Stefan said, turning around and looking over the room. "That can't be fun."

"It's fun and frustrating."

Stefan turned back to face his brother. "You keep enjoying the traffic, but let's talk seriously about what's going to happen tomorrow."

"I can't believe it. Do you think Mom didn't know he was alive all this time?"

"She didn't say much about that final attack," Stefan noted. "Only that Petre was killed and after that she worked her way to the United States."

"I hope Petre's side of that story will explain what happened."

Stefan rubbed his eyes of tears that were forming. "It just breaks my heart to think of him being alive all that time and Mom maybe not knowing it."

"You need to remember that she defected. She couldn't have had a relationship with him anyway. He might have been alive, but neither of them was ever going to be allowed to come and visit the other."

"I know," Stefan said. "It's just all so sad."

"Answers will come tomorrow," he said. Andrew looked over his glass and suddenly put it down. "Oh my Lord!"

"What's wrong?"

"Absolutely nothing. The most beautiful woman we've seen today just walked into the restaurant."

Stefan picked up his glass and casually turned. "Dark blue business suit, blonde hair?"

"Who else?"

"She's something," Stefan said, turning back to face his brother.

"She's looking all over the room," Andrew whispered. "I hope her party is somewhere in my field of vision."

Stefan smiled. "Let me point some things out. Business suit, hair in a tight bun, minimal makeup —"

"She doesn't need any!" Andrew protested.

"I'm not done and haven't made my point. Have you noticed that she's also not wearing any jewelry?"

"Alright, so what is your point?" he asked.

"Look at her shoes."

"I tried, but with those legs I never got there," Andrew said. "Alright. Flats. Very functional."

Stefan chuckled. "Don't you see the signs? That, my dear brother, is a government employee."

"So?"

"Spy Craft 101. She's Securitaté."

"You're crazy!" Andrew said. "There's absolutely no way that celestial being is one of them."

Stefan raised an eyebrow. "You're too distracted by her other attributes to notice that she's packing a weapon, Andrew."

He looked at her carefully and spotted the bulge below her left shoulder. "You're right, she is," he said. "I feel awful right now. This could be an attack and I let my guard down. It won't happen again."

"Relax," Stefan said. "We're in a restaurant. She's not going to do anything deadly."

"Do you forget where I was just two weeks ago?"

Stefan nodded. "She's coming this way."

"Let's hope she just needs to have something blessed," Andrew said.

Aurora approached their table. "Good evening, gentlemen," she said in lightly accented English. She took her badge out of her purse and held it up. "I'm Agent Zamfir with the SRI. Could I speak with you two for a moment?"

Andrew looked at his brother. "I don't happen to know what the SRI is."

Stefan smiled. "It's the modern equivalent of the communist-era Securitaté. Isn't that right, Agent Zamfir?" he asked.

"Not exactly," she replied. "I would prefer to call it the Romanian equivalent of your FBI. We are a law enforcement and intelligence agency, not Secret Police."

"Well, we're American citizens," Andrew said angrily. "And we don't have to talk to anyone we don't want to. We sure as hell aren't going to talk to some Communist agent."

She rolled her eyes and sighed. "I'm not a communist, Mr. Valquist. And you don't have to talk to me if you don't want to."

"It's actually Dr. Valquist," Stefan said.

"We do speak Romanian," Andrew said. "Don't you already know that, as well as my favorite color and the name of the first girl I ever kissed?"

"But apparently not the fact that you have a Ph.D.," Stefan said.

Aurora looked between the brothers. "I assumed that two men raised by a Romanian mother spoke at least a little of the language. But I spoke in English in case your Romanian wasn't fluent. I'll answer all your questions, gentlemen, but could I sit with you a moment?"

Andrew looked at his brother. Stefan nodded slowly.

"Take a seat, Agent Zamfir," Andrew said. "But you answer our questions first."

"Agreed," she said in Romanian, slipping into the booth beside Stefan.

"How do you know who we are?" Stefan asked.

"A fair question," she answered. "Suffice it to say that for security reasons every country keeps track of the names of people on flight logs. You aren't security risks. But your background has you flagged as significant persons whose travel to Romania is interesting to us."

"What background are you talking about?" Andrew asked.

"A mother who was a member of the Haiduci."

Andrew and Stefan locked eyes. In that moment, they had the answer to the controversy that had long strained them.

"Then it was true," Stefan whispered to his brother.

"I'll take that as a 'yes'," Aurora said.

"How did you find us here, in this restaurant?" Stefan asked her.

"Well, I assumed you would stay somewhere downtown. So, I engaged in a bit of what you people call 'pre-texting'."

"You called places and said you knew us until someone made the mistake of admitting we were there," Stefan said, sipping his wine again.

"Exactly. Then I assumed you would ask for a restaurant recommendation from the front desk. I went to the Majestic and pretended to cry and said my cell was out of power and that I was supposed to meet you two for dinner."

"And the receptionist told you where she had recommended," Andrew finished for her.

"It wasn't rocket science," she said. "Strangely, she seemed disappointed that another person would be joining your party."

"That's probably because someone went down there and pretended to practice his Romanian," Stefan said, smirking.

"Excuse me?" Aurora asked.

"Inside joke. All right, that all makes sense," Stefan continued. "Now the more important question. Why are you here?"

"And the answer to that is … exactly the same question. Why are *you* here? You two speak fluent Romanian. Why have you never visited your mother's native country until today?"

The waitress approached their table.

"Would you like something to drink, Agent Zamfir?" Stefan asked.

"No, thank you," she replied. "I'm on duty."

"Could you please come back in just a few minutes?" Andrew said.

The waitress nodded and left.

"We're not going to answer that question," Stefan said. "It's a private matter."

"That's it? Nothing more?" she asked.

"I agree with my brother," Andrew said.

Aurora stood up from the booth. "I thank you for your time. But, before I leave, I just want to tell you to be careful."

"What the hell is that supposed to mean?" Andrew said loudly. "Are you threatening us, Agent Zamfir?"

"No, I'm not threatening you. And I may even be outside my authority to be saying this much. In my book you count enough as Romanians for your security to matter to me. And that's why I'm asking you, in the interest of your safety, to be careful while you're here."

"Noted," Stefan said. "I think you better just leave now."

She quickly wrote on a piece of paper and handed it to Andrew. "Call this number if you change your mind and want to talk to me."

"Thank you," Andrew said, taking the paper and putting it in his pocket. "But don't wait by the phone."

She nodded and walked away quickly.

Andrew took a long drink from his glass. "Still hungry?" he asked.

"Surprisingly yes," Stefan said, opening the menu. He looked up at his brother. "What's going on here?"

"I wish I knew."

Andrew scanned the menu. He nodded and closed it.

"It's been over a year since I had *sarmale*," he said. "You get something else and we'll split them."

"*Snitsel*, then." Stefan refilled the glasses. "So, it would seem that Mom really was what she claimed."

"I now take that as a given," Andrew replied. He took out the piece of paper and studied it. "This just says 'Zamfir'. Did you get a first name off that badge?"

"No," Stefan said. "Why don't you call her and ask?"

"I don't talk to Securitaté," Andrew replied. He leaned forward and watched as a group of large suited men entered the front door of the restaurant. "Maybe

I'm just getting paranoid, but these guys don't look like casual diners. Check them out."

Stefan turned slowly and examined the scene. "The one on the left, the guy in black pinstripes — he's packing. But they're taking up positions like bodyguards clearing a room."

"Good observation. Could there be a dignitary arriving?"

The brothers saw dozens of flashes outside the large tinted plate glass doors. A murmur built outside as the doors opened again. Another large man in a suit entered. As he turned to one side, a tall woman with long red hair followed, a familiar low-cut and short emerald green dress clinging to her body.

"My good God in heaven," Andrew muttered.

"You recognize her, right?" Stefan asked.

"It's Vali! The billboards don't even do her justice."

Their waitress approached the table.

"What is she doing here?" Stefan asked.

"Every so often Vali comes into Bucharest night spots for brief photo ops," she said. "This isn't the first time she's been here."

Andrew watched as the singer signed autographs for a growing line of restaurant patrons. "Our lucky night," he said.

They gave their dinner orders and remained transfixed by the commotion near the door.

"You know you want to go meet her," Stefan said. "I'll be fine here."

"Are you sure?" he asked, searching his pockets. "You got a pen?"

Stefan handed him the instrument. "Under the circumstances, I won't even mind if you play your tourist bit."

"*Mulțumesc*," Andrew said, smiling through a faked American accent.

"Wait a minute," Stefan said. "Take a look!"

Andrew focused back to the front of the restaurant. "She's pointing over here," he said. "And now she's coming this way!"

One of the bodyguards arrived first. "Ms. Vali would like to speak for a moment with the good Father."

"It would be our pleasure," Stefan replied.

"Thank you," he said, and stepped aside.

Vali approached their table hesitantly. "Excuse me for interrupting your meal," she started. "A friend gave me a crucifix and, with my busy concert schedule, I just haven't had time to get it blessed."

Andrew contained a smile.

"I'd be happy to take care of that," Stefan replied. "Please sit down with us for a moment."

She slid into the booth beside Andrew, who moved over to accommodate her.

"Are you two brothers?" she asked.

"Twins, actually," Andrew said, fighting to keep his eyes from wandering off of hers.

"How special," she said, putting her hand on his shoulder. "Forgive me, but I am detecting just the tiniest accent in your Romanian. Are you from Transylvania?"

"America," Stefan said. "We grew up there but learned the language from our Romanian mother."

"She taught you very well."

"You have no idea," Andrew said. "But I'm a big fan of your music. We even listen to it there."

"You flatter me. Excuse me, but what are your names?"

"I'm Andrew. And the good priest is Stefan."

"Pleased to meet both of you," she said, shaking their hands. "What brings you to Romania?"

"We're here to visit our uncle," Andrew said.

"That's very nice." She took a golden necklace from a small purse. "Here's the item I mentioned."

"Hold it like so," Stefan said, positioning her hand above the table. As he took his small bottle of Holy Water from his pocket, he shot a glance over to Andrew, who was taking full advantage of Vali's diverted attention. He performed the blessing.

"Thank you, Father Stefan," she said, getting out of the booth. "I'm sorry, but I have to run."

They both stood from the booth as well.

"Vali, it was very nice to meet you," Andrew said. "The Romanians in America will not believe it when we tell them about this."

She kissed each of them on the cheek. "Enjoy your time here," she said, smiling and departing.

The brothers sat back down at their booth.

"I guess we can add 'Met Romania's biggest singing sensation' to our vacation log," Stefan noted.

"Think of it, meeting an SRI agent and Vali all in one night."

Stefan looked at him curiously. "SRI agent?"

"Don't say it."

"I didn't need to. That's the second time you've brought her up since she left. When a gorgeous rock star can't shake a woman out of your mind, you are officially smitten."

Andrew sipped his wine. "I'm starting to love Romania."

***

"I finished scrubbing those pots," Brother Teofil said, wiping his face with a towel. He watched as Petre quickly arranged a collection of plates on a dish rack. The old monk slid it into the machine and slammed the door down. He punched a button to begin the washing cycle and spun around, grabbing a waterspout. Without losing a second, he was spraying water into a row of dirty glasses he had set up.

"How do you do this day after day?" Teofil asked.

Petre paused a moment to sip from a glass of water. "It's the best job in the monastery."

The young man smiled. "So you've told me. You know, once they ordain me a priest, I'll never have to do anything menial again."

Petre scanned the counter and saw that no dirty dishes remained. "Thanks for your help again tonight."

"You know it's part of my punishment," Teofil countered. "Why do you keep thanking me for it?"

"Because you don't have to work with me, do you?"

"I do if I want to become a priest."

Petre looked at him seriously. "Then there it is. Something matters enough to you that you put up with the crazy monk in the dish room."

Teofil smiled. "I'm actually going to miss working with you. I've said it a dozen times now, but I really am so sorry about that joke. But at the same time, I wouldn't have gotten to know you without it."

Petre nodded. "We've had some fun here." The older monk wiped the counter with his towel and chuckled. "So when you're Patriarch of all Romania don't forget about the little guy working in the dish room."

A buzzer sounded to signal that the batch of dishes were clean. The young monk pulled up the door and slid the steaming hot rack from the machine. He carefully picked off the plates and began to stack them.

"Tomorrow's my last day with you," Teofil said. "I'd like to request this duty again, Brother." He finished stacking the dishes and set the pile onto a cart next to the dish machine. "But you and I both know that they want me to concentrate on my theological studies more."

"God bless you in your future ministry," Petre said, looking at the counter. "Remember me whenever you eat from a clean plate."

Teofil laughed and pushed the cart out of the dish room. He began the task of stacking the plates in the cabinet over the main stove. He was lifting a load of plates above his head when the shelf suddenly gave way.

Petre heard the sound and lunged toward him. He pulled Teofil down and shielded him from the onslaught of falling ceramic with his own body. Both men screamed as a seemingly endless crash of plates continued. When finally the clamor subsided, Petre lifted himself to inspect the scene. He rubbed away a trickle of blood running down from a cut on his head.

"Are you alright?" Teofil asked the older monk.

"I'm fine," Petre said, laughing. "That sure takes me back."

"To where?"

Petre put his arm around Teofil's shoulder and led him back to the dish room. "Just between you and me, there was a time when my life was a bit more complicated than morning prayers and stacks of dishes."

The young monk shook his head. "My heart's pounding," he said. "Didn't that scare you?"

"Yes, it did. But I did what I had to do for the future Patriarch."

"I think you saved my life," Teofil said. "Are you sure you're alright?"

"I am," the old monk said. Petre breathed deeply through his nose and exhaled. "I even feel like my mind's a little clearer."

Chapter Eleven

"I have to admit, I'm pretty impressed with this Metro system," Stefan said, looking over their half-filled subway car.

"Mom didn't tell us the Communists could make anything so nice as this," Andrew said. "Just like she never told us there could be such a thing as an attractive Securitaté agent."

Stefan looked at his brother and grinned. "You do know that's the fourth time you've mentioned her this morning?"

"Well, you can rest assured that, even were the opportunity to present itself, I draw the line at Communists and Securitaté."

A scratchy recording called out an approach to the Obor Station.

"That's us, right?" Stefan asked.

"Yes," Andrew said. "From there to the monastery is just a fifteen minute walk northeast."

The subway train slowed to a halt. The brothers struggled to get off the car as a crowd of people pushed their way on.

"No one taught them to wait their turn?" Andrew said.

"It's something I think is still ingrained from the years under communism. If you don't push your way into things, you won't get what's coming to you."

"Fifteen years should have mellowed them a bit," Andrew stated, looking at the signs hanging from the ceiling. "There's the exit," he said, pointing the way.

"I've got a lot of parishioners who lived in Romania during that time," Stefan said, following his brother toward an escalator. "They say some habits will take two generations to fade away."

"The Communists sure did a number on these people."

Stefan stopped his brother. "I also know a lot of people who were members of the Party simply because they had to be. You could lighten up a bit on just spouting Mom's mantras about them being pure evil."

"I know," he said. "And in retrospect I was a bit unfair to that Securitaté agent last night."

Stefan smiled. "Fifth time."

Andrew continued walking. "I can't believe we're about to meet Petre," he said.

"I know. I feel so nervous all of a sudden. What will he be like?"

The two entered a large open area of the station bustling with stores and colorful kiosks on every side. Thirty feet up an escalator, opaque glass windows set in concrete were shining down a silvery light from the surface. Walking in silence, they studied the scene carefully.

"Check out the guy leaning against the wall on your left," Stefan whispered. "I swear he looked at us as if he were expecting us."

"I already had him," Andrew returned. "What about your two o'clock? Black suit."

"Shit!" Stefan muttered. "I'm sorry. A priest shouldn't swear. At least not like that. You see that bulge under his coat? He's wearing a piece! What is this?"

Andrew stopped and pretended to tie his shoe. Stefan pretended to stand relaxed and waiting for him.

"This could be connected to our visitor last night," Andrew said softly.

"They're not just on surveillance here," Stefan returned. "From their placement, they're planning an action on us."

Andrew stood up, quickly studying his brother's point. "I agree," he said. "As sure as our training taught us, at least two, probably more, are about to do something."

"Their array looks like a kidnapping to me," Stefan said. "I also think their placement implies a third who would be at your current nine o'clock."

Andrew looked up nonchalantly. "Good call. He's there."

"I can't see a fourth anywhere," Stefan said.

"And that means —"

"Three men aren't kidnapping two. They intend to kill one of us and kidnap the other."

"Agreed," Andrew said, starting to walk again slowly. "Our liabilities are that we have no weapons whatsoever. What's the plan?"

"Do I need to remind you that another of our liabilities is that, as a priest, I can't take a human life?" Stefan whispered urgently.

"I know."

"Look," Stefan said. "Except for that incident at the store, I've never faced a crisis. I'm scared out of my wits right now."

"That makes two of us," Andrew said.

"Okay, a plan," Stefan said. "Can it include me not killing?"

"Let's hear it."

"You were always the gun guy, but I have you on the hand-to-hand combat."

"True enough."

"We can't fight and knock out three armed men. Walk with me to that kiosk."

Andrew followed his brother toward a stall surrounded by trays of various fruits.

"Does it matter that these guys might be Romanian Securitaté agents?" Stefan asked.

"I don't care if they're Rotarians," Andrew said. "They intend us harm. We can't just let that happen without a fight."

"And a pre-emptive strike? Are we so sure about their intentions to kill?"

Andrew sighed. "Well that's the thing, isn't it? What if we do nothing and get killed?"

"We do it," Stefan whispered. He turned to the woman behind the counter. "How much for the apples?" he asked.

"One *leu* each," she said.

"Here you are," Stefan replied, handing her two singles and picking up two green apples. He turned and began walking slowly back toward the exit.

"I see where this is going," Andrew whispered, catching up to his brother.

"I need you to make a commotion. That will take away their element of surprise. I'm going to stun the wall guy and get his gun off him. I'll throw it across the corridor to the spot that will be my two o'clock from that point. After that I'll try to hide behind the guy I immobilized. Hopefully they'll hesitate from firing on us just long enough for you to take control of the gun."

"I don't remember this maneuver," Andrew said.

"I just made it up. It's called 'A Wing and a Prayer' because if it works it'll be a miracle. But it's better than doing nothing."

"Understood."

"Can you try to just injure them?" Stefan asked.

"Not really," Andrew said. "That's just in the movies. If I have to stop a man with a gun, I aim at his midsection. If I try to shoot his legs and —"

"I know, I know," Stefan said. "God, I just can't believe this is happening. Alright, on one."

"Listen," Andrew said. "We've never been in danger together before."

"I love you," Stefan said. "No matter what happens, know that."

"I love you, too." Andrew took a deep breath. "We don't have time for the prayer. But we mentioned it and that's enough. One on your mark."

"Five, four, three, two, one ..."

Andrew threw his arms in the air and began screaming at the top of his lungs, running a circle through the area.

Stefan took one of the apples and threw it with his entire strength. It exploded directly on his target's face. The man collapsed against the wall. Stefan rushed toward him and struck him hard across the jaw to ensure he was unconscious. He slipped his hand inside the man's jacket.

Andrew stopped his noise and began a sprint to the spot his brother had indicated.

Stefan hurled the gun away, not even looking for his brother's position.

As Andrew ran, he saw the gun flying through the open space. Calculating that his speed would not be enough, he dove forward. Horizontal to the ground, his fingers managed to seize the sailing gun.

Stefan pulled the unconscious man in front of him. Looking back and forth between the two other assailants, he saw that one of them was just pulling out his gun to fire on Andrew. The other was already aiming carefully and directly into Stefan's eyes. Stefan saw that the man was well trained and was about to take the shot. He watched the entire scene unfolding as if in slow motion, so heightened were his senses with the terror of the moment.

"Your eleven o'clock!" Stefan shouted.

Andrew tumbled to the ground as he positioned the weapon in his hand. He raised his sights to the target and squeezed off a shot. A spray of blood filled the scene as the assailant convulsed and began to fall. Andrew swung his sight over to the other target and saw that the man had taken full aim on his position.

"*Damn*," Andrew thought. He expected the attacker to get off the first shot, but instead saw a green apple explode in the man's face. The assailant fired his gun as he fell to the ground. Andrew heard the shot ricochet harmlessly behind him.

Only then did the brothers hear people screaming all around them over what had happened. They saw a police officer in a light blue uniform down the hall blowing a whistle and running toward them.

"Let's just drop to the ground here," Stefan said. "This officer could do anything under pressure."

"I know," Andrew said, stretching out his arms and kneeling.

The two brothers lay on their stomachs facing each other as various jurisdictions of law enforcement emerged and immobilized them.

"We can add 'attacked in a Bucharest subway' to our vacation log," Stefan joked, tears flowing from his eyes.

"But I'll bet we at least get a free prison meal out of this," Andrew said, smiling gently.

As an officer roughly threw handcuffs on him, Stefan looked at his brother.

"Well done," Andrew said.

***

"Tell me what we know right now," the director said, settling back at his desk.

"I'm still pulling the information in," Aurora said. "Agent Bucur is the man who was killed."

"Damn it," he said, slamming his fist on the desk. "This is exactly what I was afraid of. We still don't know what these Americans are doing in Romania?"

"As I told you, they won't speak to me because they see me as a modern version of what their mother fought."

"What about the other men? They aren't SRI. Who the hell are they?"

"We have no information on them and they're not speaking. The only reason we identified Bucur is that his fingerprints matched the ones in our security records."

The director looked out the window. "How did two unarmed Americans survive an attack by three men, one of them a highly trained intelligence officer?"

"I'm still analyzing the scene to figure that out. Witnesses report that the priest attacked the men with apples."

The director looked at her in confusion. "Apples against handguns and they won?"

Aurora smiled. "Yes, sir. It would seem their mother taught them more than just Romanian. If I could point out some good news, with Bucur dead, we have no reason to believe that there is currently a SABIA presence in our building."

"I would agree with you," he said. "And what do you conclude from that?"

"I have a theory I'm still working through," she said. "What if SABIA is not actually as big as we once thought?"

"Go on."

"It doesn't make sense to waste someone as valuable as a mole inside the SRI on something like an assassination attempt against two Americans."

"But Bucur was no longer in access of classified information. Maybe they figured in this specific instance they needed his weapons skills more than the potential of getting him back into the building."

"But wouldn't even that suggest that they don't have a large number of weapons experts?"

He nodded slowly. "Good point. So if SABIA is short staffed, why do they attack two American tourists who just happen to be the sons of a Haiduci fighter?"

"The Americans still hold the key to that," she said. "I would like to offer them access to our information in exchange for what they know."

He was silent in contemplation. "I don't think that's a good idea," he finally said.

"Sir, I know this has plenty of pros and cons. But with the death of Bucur, we have no leads left. The only people who know something which undoubtedly figures into this puzzle are those two Americans."

"Now don't you wish you could use thumbscrews?" he said, chuckling.

She momentarily did not know how to respond. "Sir, we need to take a risk here. We certainly know that the Americans aren't part of SABIA. They're the very antithesis of it. And the war between the Haiduci and SABIA has now had a battle in Bucharest. So if they can point us in a new direction, giving them our information will be worth it."

"You're the one in charge of this investigation," he said. "Do what you think is right."

* * *

Andrew and Stefan sat alone at a large table in a conference room at the American Embassy. The beige painted walls around them were adorned with pictures of famous American landmarks. They turned and watched as the only door to the room suddenly opened.

"Good evening, gentlemen," a gray-suited African-American man said, entering and closing the door behind him. "I'm Jack Williams, the FBI Liaison attached to this Embassy."

"Hello," Stefan returned. "Could you tell us when we'll be able to leave? As you know, this has been a terribly long day for us."

"Indeed it has," he said, sitting down at the table across from the brothers. He slid a sheet of paper over to them. "Here's a summary of the statement you already made to the Bucharest Police. Please read this over and let me know if there is anything you would like to change."

Andrew positioned the paper between himself and his brother. "On vacation in Romania," he read in a mumble. "Observed that three men were about to ambush us ... took appropriate measures of self defense."

"That's accurate enough," Stefan said.

Agent Williams sat back in his chair. "You know, if it weren't for the fact that Stefan is an Orthodox priest in an Orthodox country, you two would probably still be in prison over this incident. And, I think the SRI was very generous to release you to my custody without interrogating you first."

"Securitaté, yes," Andrew said. "We know all about them."

"As a law enforcement agent, the SRI are my colleagues here. We have an intelligence sharing relationship. Romania is a democratic country now, Dr. Valquist. It's not 1975 and those people are not your enemies."

"You really don't know our family that well," Andrew snapped.

"What's this attitude?" he asked. "Can't you see that I'm trying to help you?"

Andrew and Stefan looked at each other seriously.

"I apologize for my brother," Stefan said. "We're understandably a bit short tempered right now."

Agent Williams nodded. "Andrew," he said carefully. "The man you killed was an SRI agent."

"I'm not surprised to hear that," he replied. "We were as much as told last night by Securitaté that they were about to do something against us."

"Andrew," Stefan said impatiently. "Let's please start referring to today's agency as SRI. Calling them Securitaté is needlessly simplistic."

Williams looked back and forth between the brothers.

"Stefan, just because you have a bunch of Communists at your Church doesn't mean that I'm going to buddy up to them," Andrew said.

Stefan looked at his brother with confusion.

Andrew's eyes softened. "That was way out of line," he said. "And I'm sorry."

"Apology accepted," Stefan said.

"Gentlemen," Agent Williams interrupted. "Let's please continue. You killed an SRI agent. That much is true. But they've disavowed any connection to what this man did."

"How convenient," Andrew said. "That's what you people call 'plausible deniability'."

"I believe them," Williams said. "I think this man was working for something else when he attacked you."

"And what would that be?" Stefan asked.

"I wish I could tell you everything," Williams started. "But the information I know about the situation is classified."

"As an Army sergeant I had a Secret clearance," Andrew said. "That's not enough to tell me a bit more?"

"I checked that out hoping I could brief you on it. But you only have a simple Secret clearance. That doesn't include access to Human or Signals Intelligence."

Andrew smiled to Stefan. "I knew that, too, but I was hoping to get further."

Williams chuckled. "Alright, gentlemen, you are free to go on your way. An SRI agent asked me to extend an invitation for you two to share anything further you could on these matters."

"Blonde? Great legs?" Andrew asked.

"I only spoke to her on the phone," Williams said. "In particular, she said she would like to know why you really came to Romania. She identified herself as Agent Aurora Zamfir and said you already had her contact information."

Andrew smiled at his brother. "We already had her number but now we have a first name."

"I think all that counts as six and seven," Stefan said.

"She hopes you'll assist her in the investigation as to why one of their rogue agents attacked you today," Williams said.

"Thank you," Stefan said. "We will consider it."

"I would also be very interested in knowing why you two came to Romania," Williams said. "At this point I'm responsible for you until you leave this country. I wish I knew for sure that this was an isolated incident. But I know there's something deeper here."

Stefan nodded. "Sir, I hope that, after we ourselves get this figured out, we can share more. But for the time being, you aren't cleared for it."

"You know how to reach me if you need my help," Williams said.

"Yes, sir," Andrew replied, standing from his chair.

"Let's go, brother," Stefan said. "We never did get that meal you promised."

Chapter Twelve

Andrew sipped from a glass of red wine. "Oh, that feels good," he whispered.

"What a day," Stefan said, slouching down in their booth. He took a healthy drink off his own glass. "My head is still spinning," he said, looking over the room.

Tonight's restaurant featured dark brown wood paneled walls decorated with nautical implements to accent their seafood specialty.

"Kristie's pretty upset, isn't she?" Andrew asked.

"Understandably so."

"So what's next for us here?" Andrew asked.

"Nothing." Stefan wiped his eyes and then took another fast drink. "I say we call the airline and change our tickets to leave on the first flight out tomorrow."

"Are you alright?" Andrew asked.

He took a deep breath. "Every time I shut my eyes I can see that guy aiming his gun at my face."

"What you're experiencing is normal," Andrew said.

"And what about you?"

He shrugged. "It really does get easier. I've been in enough firefights now that I can detach right after. But it'll catch up with me too."

Stefan drained his glass and topped both of them off again. "Is it a problem that I want to get so drunk that I don't see him anymore?"

"Only if you need a drink tomorrow morning," Andrew said. He looked into his own glass. "So Petre didn't really exist?"

Stefan shook his head. "But how did the guy on the phone know the prayer?"

"None of this makes any sense."

"You know I still have a lot of unanswered questions about Mom," Stefan said. "I was really hoping Petre could be a window into her."

"Good evening, gentlemen," a waitress said, arriving at their booth. "Are you ready for me to take your order?" She was tall and trim, wearing a black leather skirt and a purple blouse.

"Yes," Andrew said. He ordered an assortment of traditional Romanian appetizers and main dishes and then handed her the menus.

"Thank you," she said. "Right away."

"Wow, you're off your game," Stefan said, watching her depart.

"What do you mean?"

"As a married man, I try not to dwell on these things, but that waitress was quite attractive and you didn't even seem to notice her."

Andrew looked up and smiled weakly. "You mean the young lady that was just here? Let's see, no ring on the left hand, a dyed brunette, and B cup."

Stefan laughed. "Alright, I stand corrected."

Andrew lifted his glass of wine and then put it down quickly. "St. Nicholas of Myra!" he shouted.

"What's wrong?" Stefan asked.

"Agent Zamfir just walked in. She's looking around, probably for us. Now she's spotted your black robes and she's coming this way."

Stefan noticed his brother's rapt attention. "And?"

He smiled. "And she's dressed to kill."

"That whole exchange counts only for eight."

Stefan slid over as she approached their booth. Aurora was wearing a red dress and black high heels. Her blonde hair, previously up in a tight bun, now poured luxuriously over her shoulders in loose curls.

"Take a seat, Agent Zamfir," Stefan said. "You obviously want to talk to us and we've got some questions for you as well."

"Good evening, gentlemen," she said, sitting down next to Stefan.

"Aurora," Andrew started, emphasizing her first name. "If I might say, you were all business yesterday. Now tonight, you seem to be out on the town. What gives?"

"I've decided that I'm off duty," she said. "And because of that, I'd like a glass of what you two are having."

Andrew motioned for the waitress and ordered another carafe and glass. He leaned over the table slightly. "First off, we didn't tell anyone at the hotel where we were going. How did you find us here? Did your agents somehow plant a bug on us this morning?"

The waitress returned with the order. Aurora picked up her glass.

"Many years," she said, raising a toast.

"Good health," Stefan replied, clinking all their glasses together. "And we do deserve an answer to that question."

"Before I answer that," Aurora started. "I know that Agent Williams explained that one of those men was an SRI agent. But he was not acting officially for us. In fact, and I'm getting way out of line here, he was one of the men I had put on a temporary leave of absence."

"Why did you do that?" Stefan asked.

"I would like to tell you everything," she said. "But I can't do that unless I get something in return."

"Wait," Andrew said. "I still want to know how you found us here."

Aurora smiled. "It was quite simple. This restaurant is between your hotel and the one they recommended for you last night. But this one is actually a bit better. I guessed that you might have spotted it yesterday and decided on something different for tonight."

Andrew and Stefan looked at each other and laughed.

"That's pretty much exactly how it went," Stefan said.

"Your turn," she said. "Two sons of a great anti-communist insurgent come to Romania for the first time ever. And they're immediately attacked by ..."

Aurora stopped and looked at each of them. "What do you *think* you were attacked by?"

"Securitaté," Andrew said.

"If you mean the Securitaté your mother fought, you're not far from the truth," she said. "But if you're just attacking me again, then we're getting nowhere, Andrew."

He looked at her and bit his lower lip.

"Can I ask another question?" she said, turning to Stefan.

"Go ahead."

"How did you two fight off three armed men today?"

Stefan sipped his wine and then looked at her seriously. "Our mother taught us well."

"You two can do everything she could? I've done some research into her in old Securitaté files. At one point a team of twenty agents was sent to find and assassinate the legendary Diana and Apollo. But one by one, they all were killed or disappeared."

"You know about our uncle, too?" Andrew asked.

Aurora turned to him. "Just that he was, with her, the bane of the Communists' existence in Brasov until he was captured."

"So he really didn't die," Andrew said to Stefan.

"Your mother said he did?"

"Yes," Stefan stated. "We'd very much like to know everything your files have on him and our mother."

"I'll do you one better," Aurora said. "I'll give you access to all that archival information. I'll also give you a full briefing on why I first came to see you yesterday. But for security reasons you'll understand that can't be done in this restaurant."

"Let me guess," Andrew said. "You want us to go right into the lion's den of Securitaté headquarters."

"SRI," Stefan said.

Andrew turned to his brother. "What if all of this has been a trap? Now they're luring us into prison with the promise of information they know we'd want."

"You're being paranoid, Andrew," she said.

"I am? We were nearly killed this morning."

Aurora touched her side as she took in a deep breath. "I don't know what else I can say to convince you that SRI isn't Securitaté and that I'm personally not a communist."

Andrew noticed the way she had touched herself. "What was that?" he asked.

"What do you mean?"

"You touched your side and braced yourself before you took a deep breath. That's what a person with cracked ribs does."

Aurora looked at him seriously. "And your point?"

"What are you saying, Andrew?" Stefan asked.

"She was shot while wearing a bulletproof vest recently. I'll bet it was within two or three days?"

Aurora put her drink down. "I'm going to repeat that I'm offering to tell you both absolutely everything, but it can't be here. If you knew anything about security issues, you would understand that's not unreasonable. But if you can't get over your prejudices about me and my government, then none of us will benefit from that information exchange."

Andrew smiled gently. "I'm sorry. Something is going on here bigger than we understand. And if you were shot —"

"Then we have a common enemy," Stefan said. "Agent Zamfir, do forgive our hesitation to work with you. This is a hard psychological barrier for us to get beyond. Our mother raised us to believe that all Securitaté were unequivocally our enemy."

"I understand that."

The waitress returned with plates of food.

"If you would let me out for a moment, Aurora," Stefan said. "I'll bless the food."

Stefan performed the benediction, after which he and Andrew crossed themselves. All three sat back down.

Andrew distributed the food between three plates. "Aurora," he said. "Almost everyone in Romania is Orthodox. But you didn't cross yourself. What religion are you?"

"I don't have any religion," she said.

"Not even nominally?" Stefan asked. "I know from my Church that many Communists here still had their babies baptized out of the sheer tradition of it."

"Not my parents. Even though I don't share the ideology they had at the time, I love them very much. They were very loyal and dedicated Communists who didn't raise me to have a religion. I don't mean to insult you two, but I haven't seen much in the behavior of religious people to make me feel I'm missing anything."

Stefan nodded. "Men and women of the Church can frequently fail to live up to our higher ideals. That's not an excuse. It's a challenge for us to do better."

"Let's change the subject," Andrew said. "Let's say hypothetically that we were willing to share information with you. What would that look like?"

"I'm in charge of an important investigation. It involved the SRI agent who attacked you. It also includes a wider concern that he was part of something much bigger. I have the authority to grant each of you clearance to read all of the classified material we have. That will be primarily Romanian intelligence, but I will also make available information forwarded to us by your own government."

Stefan raised his eyebrows. "You mean you'd tell us what Agent Williams wouldn't?"

"That's right."

They continued eating over polite conversation about Romanian cuisine.

"Order us one more carafe," Stefan said, getting up from his chair. "I'll be right back."

Andrew moved over in the booth to face Aurora directly. "Tell me something," he said softly. "What happened to the guy who shot you?"

Aurora looked up at the ceiling in consideration of her words. Her eyes flooded suddenly with tears.

"You killed him," Andrew said.

"Never did I imagine I would take a human life," she said, picking up her glass and taking a drink.

"And it was your first."

She nodded without speaking.

"My first was about a year ago," he said.

"Agent Williams said you just got out of the Army and that you were in Iraq."

"I was scared out of my wits most of the time. Did you throw up after you killed your guy?"

"No," she said.

"I did. Just the thought of it. Taking someone's life. There's some mother, living or dead, it doesn't matter, who spent thousands of hours caring for that person. And in a second, you've made all that go away."

"How many has it been?" she asked.

"Five in all. And that includes your friend this morning."

She opened her mouth to protest.

"I'm sorry," Andrew said quickly. "Seriously. That was wrong and unfair. I know he wasn't your friend."

"Thank you," Aurora said.

Stefan left the bathroom and looked across the room at their table. He smiled as he watched his brother and Aurora talking. Leaning against the wall, he decided to wait a while longer before returning.

"When exactly did you get back from there?" she asked.

Andrew looked at her curiously. "You didn't receive a briefing on it?"

"I really don't have a secret dossier on you, Andrew," she said, smiling at him warmly. "I don't know your favorite color ..." She paused to take a sip of wine. "And I don't know the name of the first girl you ever kissed."

"I got back just four days ago," he said, feeling himself blush from her last statement.

"What will you do now?" she asked.

"I was a Latin teacher before the Army. I guess I'll try to find another position."

She lifted her glass and smiled. "*In vino veritas!*"

"You've obviously studied some yourself," he said.

"Latin was the key for me mastering a number of languages. I started out at the SRI as a French and Spanish linguist."

"*Tres bien,*" he said. "*Y que bueno.*"

"Will it be hard to find another job?"

"It will probably mean a longer commute, if not moving out of the state." Andrew said. "This, while I was hoping to spend more time with Stefan. But I really don't want to think about those problems until I get back there."

"I understand," she said.

They sipped at their wine and locked eyes for a long moment.

Andrew smiled at her. "I think I'm starting to trust you," he said.

"It'll be worth it, Andrew."

Stefan came back to the table. "Slide over," he said to his brother.

"It's getting late," she said. "Thank you, gentlemen, for this evening. Before I leave, I repeat my offer. If you come to SRI headquarters, I'll give you a full briefing on what you seem to have become entangled in."

"Could I ask, Aurora," Stefan began. "What do you get out of letting us know all that?"

"Potentially nothing," she replied. "But I hope, after you learn what we know, that you will help me in this investigation."

"Sounds like we have the advantage here," Andrew said.

"I've little choice," Aurora said. "I lost my only lead this morning."

Stefan wiped his mouth with his napkin and looked at his brother. Andrew nodded assent.

"We will come first thing in the morning," Stefan said.

"Good," she said. "With your permission, SRI will be placing a perimeter of security around your hotel room tonight. We don't want to see a repeat of what happened today."

"Sounds good," Andrew said. "I'll sleep easier knowing you're watching over us."

Aurora stood up from the table. "I'll have a car waiting outside your hotel at 7:00 AM which will take you to SRI headquarters. The front gate will be expecting you and you'll be able to proceed immediately through the security checks. You'll be briefed on what we know and you'll have the opportunity to share with us your information."

"And will food be provided?" Andrew asked.

"Food?"

"Yeah, we kind of got cheated on that today."

She laughed. "We will treat you as our honored guests. Don't worry."

Andrew and Stefan stood and each shook her hand.

"See you tomorrow," Andrew said, smiling.

Chapter Thirteen

The brothers sat in black leather chairs in a large conference room at SRI headquarters. A golden icon of St. George slaying a dragon filled half of the wall behind the slightly larger chair at the head of the table. A woman entered with a full coffee service, followed by a man carrying a silver tray of assorted pastries.

"If you sirs need anything further, please just let someone know," the woman said.

"Thank you," Andrew said. "This is wonderful."

Stefan took a cup of coffee poured by the woman and sipped. "Aurora wasn't kidding. If this is breakfast, lunch should be phenomenal."

The main door opened and Aurora entered with several folders. She was wearing a black business suit and had her hair back up in a bun.

"Good morning, gentlemen," she said.

"Well, good morning, Aurora," Andrew said. "If I might say, you look terrific."

She threw him a quirky smile. "Thanks. Listen, I'm going to leave you some items to read over while you relax with your coffee." She placed two identical folders in front of the twins. "These constitute in written form our current knowledge about the matters we're disclosing to you. This includes a report from your own FBI that corroborates Romanian intelligence."

"We're going to actually read Top Secret stuff?" Andrew asked. "And you don't want to hear our information first?"

"I hope that our willingness to divulge our knowledge first will contribute to establishing a level of trust between the two sides. But you may also understand the significance of your knowledge only in light of our reporting."

"Thank you, Aurora," Stefan said. "We're feeling very good about our decision to cooperate with your investigation."

"I'll come back in about an hour and we can discuss these materials. At that point, if you are willing, we would like to know your side of the story."

She left, shutting the door behind herself.

"Oh my God, she's even more gorgeous in the morning," Andrew said, putting his head on the table.

"But very professional today," Stefan stated. "Maybe even a bit distant."

"I noticed that. Every sentence from her is constructed like a legal contract."

"Do you know why?" Stefan asked.

"No."

"She's trying to establish boundaries between you two."

"What do you mean?"

"From the beginning there's been a certain chemistry, hasn't there?"

"Despite my joking, I really can't see myself with a Securitaté agent."

"You frame it as joking because you're trying to protect yourself too," Stefan said.

Andrew put his coffee down and took a deep breath. "I don't like this situation." He turned to his brother and nodded seriously. "I know what you're saying is true. But she's a stunning woman who is exactly what Mom trained us to fight. So the fact is, I don't *like* liking her."

Stefan smiled. "I'm glad that's settled. Let's get to work."

Andrew opened his folder and started to read.

***

"You've had a chance to look over all the materials," Aurora said. "Do you have any questions?"

"Do you think there are any other SABIA moles in this building past the one you suspended and Andrew killed," Stefan asked.

"At this time I have no information that would prove there has to be another mole here," she replied. "But I certainly can't rule it out either."

They nodded.

Andrew examined a page in his folder. "Your records indicate that Petre was shot during his capture and put in prison a few months later. Where was he in the meantime?"

"That's something I was going to explain verbally," Aurora answered. "Some records connected to him seem to have been destroyed. Petre spent a couple of months in the custody of a Securitaté official who was known for excessive cruelty. The man would have been prosecuted for crimes against humanity after the Revolution, but he disappeared."

"He must have truly been a nasty character," Stefan said.

"The individual in question destroyed incriminating records. All I've been able to piece together is that Petre must have been someone whose treatment was thus erased."

"And you have no further information on what happened to Petre?" Andrew asked.

"I'm sorry," she said. "I can prove he was put in prison two months after his capture. We have a record that he was released in early 1990 after the Revolution. Immediately after that, it's like he vanished."

"Why would he not have tried to contact Mom after he got out?" Stefan asked his brother.

"How?" Andrew said. "A guy who just got out of jail after almost thirty years isn't going to have the wherewithal to find someone who defected to the US like that. He probably wanted to find her but just couldn't imagine how to start."

"That's one explanation," Stefan said. "Or what if he knew that she had been killed?"

Andrew and Stefan looked at each other, each drawing the same conclusion.

"How did Doina die?" Aurora asked softly.

"Our parents were rear ended in an accident and then hit a tree," Andrew responded. "That's all the cops knew from the scene."

"And they never found the other vehicle, right?"

The brothers nodded.

"That's one *modus operandi* of an assassination by Secret Police," Aurora said, looking between Andrew and Stefan. "I'm so sorry."

"Actually, I find peace in that thought," Andrew said. "It makes it somehow less senseless."

"If someone had told Petre that they killed Doina, that would explain why he never tried to contact her," she said. "But we don't know that's what actually happened." Aurora poured herself a cup of coffee and took a sip. "You've learned what we know. Now, why did you two come to Romania?"

"I thought you'd never ask!" Andrew said.

The brothers explained in detail their contact with a man claiming to be Petre and their trip up to the point they had met Aurora. When they had concluded their account, all three sat in silent contemplation.

"This is certainly a strange turn," she finally said. "What are the logical possibilities?"

"It could be that it really was Petre who tried to contact us," Andrew started. "And somehow SABIA found out about it and attacked us before we could meet him."

"That's possible," Stefan said. "But it doesn't ring true for me. Why would SABIA not want us to meet Petre? How could they find out about him contacting us in the first place? Why were they apparently trying to kidnap one of us?"

"But how could SABIA have known about the prayer if it was someone besides Petre who contacted you?" Aurora asked.

"They could have tortured it out of Petre," Andrew said.

Aurora stood up from her chair and paced next to the table. Andrew began unconsciously studying her as she walked. Stefan jabbed his elbow in his brother's ribs to distract him.

"There are a lot of possible universes here," she finally said. "But how's this? SABIA wasn't after you two at all. They're after Petre himself."

"You're saying Petre is still alive?" Andrew asked. "Even so, how could he possibly matter so much to SABIA that they wanted to get to him?"

Stefan sat back in his chair. "This makes sense to me," he said. "SABIA supposedly has this massive attack coming. They may expect their plans to advance quickly after that. Somehow Petre could be a loose end. Even at this late hour they are willing to resort to desperate measures to get him."

"But where is he?" Andrew asked.

"It makes sense that he really could be at that monastery," Stefan said. "It's not very far from the prison he stayed at. We know he'd have been a man of faith, judging from our mother. With nowhere else to go, a monastery would have been a good choice. It's also a place one could vanish into."

Andrew smiled. "They didn't expect us to fight back the way we did, so they didn't realize the harm in letting us know that information."

"In fact," Aurora said, "if Petre's at that monastery, letting you know it was an amateurish error on their part. And that would play into a theory I'm working through. I'm starting to think that SABIA is not nearly as big and organized as they want us believe."

"But wouldn't it be a simple matter to just send an assassin into a monastery to kill a monk?" Andrew asked.

"It's not as easy as it sounds," Stefan said. "There would be no way to get a schematic of who is where at any given time. A monk's quarters would be unmarked. Sending someone into a monastery to kill a specific person would be like finding a needle in a haystack."

"I see what you're saying," Andrew said. "But having one of his long lost nephews in their custody would change everything. They could have used one of us as bait to draw him out of safety."

The three looked at each other with increasing excitement.

"But I still don't see how Uncle Petre could be that important," Stefan said. "This would almost imply that somehow Petre is related to the very constitution of SABIA itself."

Andrew stood up. "I think only Uncle Petre, if he really is there, can answer that question."

Aurora took out her cell phone and dialed a number. "I want a level two security perimeter put around *Sfânta Treime* Monastery immediately," she said. "I'll explain the matter when I arrive there in fifteen minutes."

***

Aurora showed her badge to a row of agents standing guard beside black BMW's at the front gate of the monastery. The three walked past the vehicles and approached twenty-foot high wooden doors set in the vine encrusted stone wall surrounding the compound. A man dressed in a long black cassock opened the door and stepped out.

"Please let us know what's going on here," the monk said. "We were told that no one could enter or leave until further notice."

"I'm the officer in charge, Father," Aurora said.

"He's not a priest," Stefan whispered.

"Then what do I call him?" she whispered back.

"Call him 'Brother'."

"Brother, I'm Agent Zamfir of the SRI," she said, showing him her badge. "We need to speak with whomever ... um ..."

"Ask for the Staretz," Stefan whispered.

"What's a Staretz?"

"The head of a monastery. It's like Abbot in the Western Church."

She smirked at him. "Thanks. Later on you can tell me what an Abbot is."

He laughed. "Aurora, you're doing great."

"Brother, I need to see the Staretz, please."

The monk nodded and disappeared behind the doors. Almost immediately, a thin and elderly man in a similar black cassock but wearing a square black hat stepped out.

"That would be the Staretz," Stefan whispered.

"I'm Staretz Teodosie," the man said. "I've been expecting you."

"How did you know we were coming?" Andrew said.

"I dreamt last night of three visitors to the monastery. How can I help you?"

Stefan stepped forward. "I'm Father Stefan Valquist," he said.

Following the custom between priests, each kissed the other's hands and then each other's cheeks.

"You speak our language, but your name's not Romanian," the Staretz said. "Are you from America?"

"Yes," he said. "But I'm not here on official Church business. My brother and I are looking for our uncle. We hope he is here at your monastery."

"What's your uncle's name?"

Andrew stepped forward and kissed the Staretz on the hand.

"Do you have a monk named Petre here?" he asked. "He's the brother of our deceased mother Doina. He'd be almost seventy years old. And he would have arrived here in 1990."

The Staretz put his hand to his mouth. "Lord have mercy," he gasped.

***

The Staretz pulled his chair up close to Petre's.

"What's going on?" Petre asked. "Is something wrong?"

"Nothing's wrong. Nothing at all." The Staretz smiled at him. "Close your eyes and pray with me for a moment. Then we're going into my office for you to meet some people."

Petre closed his eyes. "Lord have mercy," he said. "Will it be too cold to ..." He clenched his eyes tightly. "I'm sorry."

"It's alright, Brother." The Staretz stood up from his chair. "Just relax. I'm going to be right next to you."

Petre looked up at him with confusion. "Why am I scared?"

"Because something's different. But it's going to be fine, alright?"

Petre stood and swallowed. "Who are these people? Are they Secret Police?"

The Staretz laughed. "Of course not! Look, let's just go in there now."

He opened the door and led Petre into his office.

Andrew and Stefan stood from chairs and looked at the elderly man with nervous smiles.

"Who are they?" Petre asked.

The Staretz gently guided Petre into the room and toward a chair.

Aurora leaned against a wall and took in the scene. She rubbed tears from her eyes as she realized the import of the moment for Andrew and Stefan.

"Petre," the Staretz said. "You told me you had a sister Doina. But now I've learned what you and she did up there near Brasov."

He looked up and immediately convulsed in grief. "I wanted so many times to tell you about it," he sobbed. "Please believe me."

"Oh my God," Andrew whispered. "It's really him."

"It's alright, Brother," the Staretz said. "It's time for you to know the peace you said could not happen in this world. Petre, these men are Doina's sons." He turned and raised his hand toward the twins. "These are your nephews, Andrew and Stefan."

Petre looked at them frantically.

"What is this?" he shouted. "Some kind of communist trick to get me to talk?" He got up from his chair and put his head in his hands.

"Don't worry," the Staretz said to the brothers. "He's very scared right now."

"What happened to him?" Andrew asked.

"I don't know," the Staretz said, looking at him with worry. "Petre, please sit back down and rest a moment."

Petre studied Andrew and Stefan. "Who are you?" he whispered.

"I'm Doina's son," Andrew said, his voice beginning to falter. "She went to America. She got married there."

"Lies!" he shouted. "They told me they killed my sister. They would have killed any sons she had."

"For some reason they didn't!" Andrew said.

"And you!" Petre shouted, pointing a finger toward Stefan. "How dare you masquerade as a priest? This is blasphemy!"

"Uncle, I am a priest and I am your nephew," Stefan said, tears now streaming down his face.

Petre moved to stand close to Stefan. "You say you're Doina's son?" he asked him angrily.

"Yes."

A look of deep rage came across his face. "Then prove it," he said.

Suddenly Petre had thrown a rapid punch. Stefan reacted instantly. The sound of a sharp slap filled the room as he stopped the fist just before his face.

Petre looked at Stefan in confusion. "My good God," he sobbed, pulling his nephew into an embrace. Andrew put his arms around them both. The three men held each other and wept.

***

"He's asleep," Andrew said, stepping out of his uncle's room.

"I would feel more comfortable if he were at SRI headquarters tonight," Aurora said.

"This is what he wanted after such a big day," the Staretz said. "He's had enough shocks to his system without also spending the night somewhere different."

"Then we're at least leaving that security detachment in place," she said.

"Will worshippers be allowed in tomorrow morning?" Stefan asked. "It's Sunday Liturgy. They probably get a couple hundred people here. You can't just shut them down."

Aurora nodded. "Staretz, I'm going to give you a choice. You can open your doors for Sunday Liturgy as usual or have Petre on these premises. But not both."

"That's fair," the Staretz replied. "Can you come and pick him up in the morning and then return him later?"

"Absolutely," she said. "Have him ready for departure at 8 AM." She turned to Andrew and Stefan. "I do insist that you two accept SRI accommodations tonight. Your belongings will be brought to our headquarters by the time we get there. You've become too important to my investigation for me to take 'no' for an answer."

Andrew smiled. "Agreed, Agent Zamfir."

Chapter Fourteen

Andrew, Stefan, and Aurora sat in the briefing room at SRI headquarters, finishing up a dinner ordered in for them. She refilled Andrew's empty wine glass.

"Thank you," he said. "I still can't believe what happened today."

Aurora put her hand atop his. "I can't imagine how emotional that was for you two."

"Now we need to figure out what all this means," Stefan said. "A massive attack is set to take place somewhere in Romania. Our only credible lead is the mystery of why SABIA wanted to get to Petre."

"How could he be so dangerous to them?" Aurora asked. "Could it be something he knows?"

"More like something he once knew," Andrew said. "He admits that he has no memory from the time he was captured until about a year later."

Aurora sipped her wine and looked down in careful thought. "If he'd share what exactly happened that night in more detail, it might help him remember," she said.

"He spent fifteen years not telling his own Staretz who he was," Andrew said. "It's going to take some time for him to open up."

"But time is what we don't have," Stefan said, swirling wine in his glass.

"Somehow Petre is a loose end for SABIA," Aurora said. "But why assassinate your mother a few weeks before the fall of communism?"

"Poland, Czechoslovakia, and East Germany had already fallen," Andrew noted. "The writing was on the wall for communism. But sending assassins into the United States was pretty daring, especially at that time."

"Killing her in that context makes no strategic sense," Aurora said.

"It's not strategic," Stefan said. "Then it would seem to be personal."

They all looked at each other with mutual understanding of the implication.

"The Securitaté interrogator," Aurora said. "She got away that night. And he wanted to get back at her while he still could. And he must somehow be related to the modern phenomenon of SABIA."

"What more do we know about this man?" Andrew asked.

Aurora raised her eyebrows. "I looked into him when I was first researching your family. Reports of his excessive cruelty were recorded in one of the hospital files. But the man himself, even his name, was somehow completely purged from all records of the Securitaté before Ceausescu was killed."

"Could he have done that himself just prior to his disappearance?" Stefan asked. "Perhaps he was trying to hide all the evidence of what he had done?"

170

"No," Aurora replied. "He would have needed help on that. Someone who stayed on the inside was involved."

"Here's a possible scenario," Andrew started. "He was one of the people who decided to prepare for an eventual insurgency against the newly democratic Romania. Part of that was to disappear from the records. The guy probably assumed a new identity so he could operate after the Revolution."

Aurora drummed her fingers on the table. "If that interrogator were alive today he'd be older than Petre. Probably he's dead by now. Who else would still have such a personal vendetta against your family?"

"How about one of his sons?" Stefan stated.

"This sounds right," Aurora said. "They didn't kill Petre when they had the chance, but decided later that Petre knows or knew something that could be dangerous."

"This idea does explain everything else we know," Stefan said. "The man was able to use his connections and maybe money secured during communism to promote his son's career. And now this son, the secret leader of SABIA, is getting ready to launch a major attack. But the loose end of Petre still worries him."

"But it still all comes down to Petre," Andrew said. "His contact with that interrogator is the missing piece of the puzzle. And he doesn't remember a bit of it."

Stefan stood from the table. "If you two will excuse me," he said. "It's been a difficult day and I'm suddenly

171

feeling very tired. I'm going to my quarters to call Kristie and John, and then turn in for the night."

"We'll talk more about all this in the morning," Aurora said.

"Sounds good."

Andrew stood and embraced his brother.

"We can add 'Met our long lost Uncle Petre but also stumbled into a web of international intrigue' to our vacation list," Stefan said.

"And I'll add 'Couldn't imagine going through this without you'," Andrew whispered. "I'll see you in the morning."

***

Andrew and Aurora relaxed on a sofa in the briefing room with what they determined had to be the last bottle of the night.

"Tell me something," she said softly. "Could you have stopped Petre's punch?"

Andrew considered the question. "I doubt it," he replied. "Honestly, I was surprised at how fast he threw that fist!"

She sipped her wine. "Then thank God it was Stefan who faced him today."

"God?" he said, grinning to her.

"You know those are expressions people use. But if you had asked me two days ago to describe a priest, I would not have come up with someone as sincere and genuine as Stefan."

"He's a credit to the clergy."

"It really is getting late, Andrew," she said. "We should get some sleep."

"I know."

The two sat in silence, neither of them wanting to formally terminate the evening.

"Let's just be adults about this situation," Aurora finally said. "I'll admit that I was thrilled when your brother went to bed early. I knew that was going to give us some time alone."

"I'm pretty sure he did that deliberately," Andrew said.

She chuckled. "It's important to acknowledge that intense experiences can affect people's perception." She turned toward him. "It can create a sense of accelerated familiarity."

"I know what you're saying, Aurora," he said, setting his wine down and putting his arm on the couch behind her shoulder. "Right now it seems like we've been doing this thing for a week, but I only met you two nights ago."

"You and I have each been shot or shot at in the last seventy-two hours," she said, leaning her head back against his shoulder. "And for the first time since I really thought I might die, I'm able to relax with someone who understands that experience."

"I just got back from Iraq only to come to Eastern Europe days later," he said, turning his head to look down into her eyes.

"And that's when things really got crazy," she said. "Now we've found ourselves thrown together for an investigation into a secret Communist group."

"I met a long lost uncle whom I believed dead but who now is our only lead toward thwarting an imminent terrorist attack."

They looked at each other and laughed at the ludicrous list of events.

"As I said, let's just be adults and state the obvious," Aurora whispered. "I enjoy being with you, Andrew."

He nodded slowly. "I feel the same way."

"We are a man and a woman experiencing a strong emotional bond because of our common backgrounds and experiences."

"Yes."

"And that only compounds the normal and intense physical attraction we're feeling in this moment."

"Indeed."

"It would be so easy right now to just surrender ourselves to it."

"Yes," he said, leaning in closer to her.

"And release all the tension our lives have thrust upon us."

"Yes," he said breathlessly.

"But we also know we shouldn't complicate this any further."

Andrew opened his mouth to speak but had no response. He finally nodded in reluctant agreement.

Then Aurora put her hand behind his neck and pulled him into a deep kiss. They lingered in it and had just begun to explore each other with caresses when they sat back on the couch.

"I needed to do that, Andrew. But that also needs to be the end of it."

He picked up his wine glass and sipped from it deeply. "If SABIA were gone, could that maybe happen again?"

"I would hope so."

He looked at her seriously. "I'll hold you to that, Agent Zamfir."

She stood from the sofa and smiled. "Sleep well, Dr. Valquist."

Chapter Fifteen

The Staretz sat in the spacious monastery dining room with Petre. Monks and priests bustled around them, preparing for the Sunday Liturgy and the large lunch to follow it.

"They'll be here in just a few minutes, Brother," the Staretz said. "It's just for today. They'll bring you back later so you can sleep here tonight. Do you understand?"

Petre looked down at a cup of coffee and a plate of eggs they had prepared for him. Since he would not be attending the Liturgy and receiving Communion, he had not needed to fast as was customary. Even so, he had only picked at the food. "I'll see my nephews again?"

"Yes. They'll be with you at all times."

He sipped his coffee. "I feel good today, Staretz. I slept better than I have in a long time. My mind feels clearer than usual."

"Excellent!" The Staretz smiled and put his hand on Petre's shoulder. "Listen, Brother, I had a dream about you last night."

"Tell me, please!" Petre returned with a huge smile.

The Staretz carefully planned his words and tried not to show any negative emotion. "You were on a trip somewhere up north. And you were happy."

"Anything else?"

"Just make a promise, alright?"

"What is it, Staretz?"

"Be very careful when you aren't here at the Monastery."

"You're saying this because of something in the dream?" Petre asked.

"No," the Staretz said quickly, feeling a tug inside at the lie. "Just in general. Be very careful when you aren't here because you've spent years without seeing the outside world. A lot has changed."

Two men in gray suits peeked into the dining room. The Staretz nodded to them.

"Go with these men now."

"Yes," Petre said.

He and the Staretz stood from their chairs. Petre took a deep breath and then smiled.

"You're a terrible liar, you know that?" he said.

"A monk shouldn't be good at it," the Staretz replied sadly.

Petre kissed him on each cheek and then pulled him into an embrace. "Staretz, you gave me a home when I didn't know where else to go," he whispered. "For everything you ever did for me, I thank you. God bless you. And good bye."

The old priest sobbed and shook his head. Petre turned and left the room.

Brother Teofil had watched the scene and approached the Staretz. "Is something wrong with Brother Petre?" he asked anxiously. "Where's he going?"

The Staretz drew a breath in slowly, trembling with grief. "Brother Petre has to leave us now."

"But when's he coming back?"

The Staretz looked at the door. "I'm afraid that he won't."

***

"Good morning," Stefan said, looking up from the briefing papers as his twin entered the room.

Andrew poured a coffee from the service and sat down next to his brother.

"I really was tired last night," Stefan said. "But at the same time ... Well? How did things go?"

"She's really something."

"I believe I said that the first moment we each laid eyes on her."

"Not the Securitaté our mother warned us about," Andrew said.

"So what's the problem?"

"The problem is that we're in the middle of an important investigation. She and I agree that we can't pursue anything else in these circumstances."

Stefan nodded. "This situation can't be easy for either of you, then."

Andrew blew on his coffee and took a sip. "Like it or not, our mentally uncertain uncle is the only hope to stop a massive attack on Romania. And you and I are the only ones he trusts outside that monastery."

"Don't remind me," Stefan said. "I woke up this morning and for just a second I could imagine everything that happened the last two days was a dream. You went to Iraq and faced serious dangers. As for me, I went to seminary."

Andrew laughed. "Well, first off, you've performed brilliantly under pressure."

"That's just the training showing through."

"Just the training? That's the whole point. When the moment of truth finally came, you put it all together. Don't minimize what you've done. Everyone who trains before any performance can never really know what will happen when they face the real thing. You learned something very important about yourself. And you should just give yourself a little credit for that."

He smiled. "Thank you. It actually does mean a lot to hear you say that."

The door opened and Aurora entered. Pouring a coffee, she sat down at the table with them.

"Good morning," Andrew said, struggling to sound normal.

She looked at him for a moment before speaking. "Good morning. I just spoke to one of our agents at the monastery. Petre is on his way here and will arrive shortly."

"Good," Andrew said.

"We'll be joined in just a moment by my boss, Mr. Gheorghe Marinescu, the director of the SRI. He wants to hear our plan for how to proceed from here."

"I guess we better come up with one, then," Stefan said.

The door opened quickly. Marinescu walked in and immediately sat at the head of the table.

"You two would be Andrew and Stefan Valquist," he said. "I'm Director Marinescu. I want to thank you both for helping clarify what went on between yourselves and our rogue agent."

"You're welcome, sir," Stefan said. "We want to assist you any way we can."

"Thank you," he replied. "I don't think we need any further help from here."

Andrew and Stefan caught each other's gaze and reacted with surprise at the slight.

The director turned to Aurora. "I've read your report about yesterday's developments. What's the current status of your investigation? I've got to report to the President on whether there's going to be an attack in Romania."

"We have no reason to doubt our previous intelligence. As for how imminent that attack might be, it would be pure conjecture."

"I would say it's somewhat imminent," Andrew said. "The attempt to get to Petre through us implies that SABIA has an increasing OPS tempo."

The director looked at him coldly. "I thank you and your brother again for the information you've provided. But it's time for you both to end any active involvement in this investigation."

Aurora swallowed hard. "Sir, I feel Andrew and Stefan remain crucial to our prosecuting the only active lead. Petre will trust them much more than he would us. Only Andrew and Stefan can help us find out what Petre may know."

He looked at her seriously. "I was pleased that you took ownership of this position. But we've now entered into a delicate spot. I don't believe you're handling this correctly. This is precisely what I didn't want to see, two American anti-communist vigilantes interfering with an important investigation."

Aurora straightened herself in her chair. "Sir, as director you can remove me from this case but for as long as I'm in charge of it, I'm going to proceed as I believe is appropriate. I'm not going to continue in charge while accepting micromanagement of my decisions."

He shook his head. "With responsibility also comes accountability, Agent Zamfir. You have the right to remove *yourself* from this case. But if you don't, you'll have to answer for whether your conduct of it was correct."

"Until you say otherwise, I'm in charge and I stand by my decisions. Andrew and Stefan are basically my deputies."

"That's your call. So what's your plan from here?"

Aurora looked at the brothers. "I haven't yet had time to discuss this with my American colleagues," she started. "But I propose that the three of us take Petre to visit the places where he lived and fought just prior to his memory gap. Perhaps the presence of his nephews and seeing that region again after all these years will help him recuperate his memory."

"That's smart," Stefan said.

"We have to try something," Andrew said. "Especially if the attack is imminent."

The director stood from his chair. "This at least lets me tell the President we're actively pursuing a response to this crisis. Make it so." He left the room without a further word.

The three sat in silence for a moment.

"You're really out on a limb to keep us involved in this," Stefan said. "Thanks for your confidence."

She smiled. "Well, none of us could have predicted a road trip with your uncle even yesterday morning. All right, Stefan, how about you head downstairs and greet Petre as he arrives. I want him as calm as possible."

"Good call," he said.

"Andrew, you and I need to check some things out of the armory. If you're my deputies, we need to get you properly supplied."

***

"How do you feel today, Uncle?" Stefan asked, kissing Petre on both cheeks.

"I'm good," he said. "We're traveling north today, right?"

Stefan looked at him, puzzled. "Yes, we are, Uncle," he said. "How did you know?"

"God is great," Petre said, putting his hand on his nephew's shoulders.

"Are you hungry?" Stefan asked.

"I am, suddenly," Petre replied. "Let us eat, for the journey is long."

***

Aurora and Andrew stood at the SRI armory, looking over a row of pistols on a counter before the young attendant in charge. The room was a broad space, almost over illuminated with rows of neon lights above. Lines of tables were set up for agents to sort their supplies before missions. The faint odor of gunpowder hung over the space.

Aurora checked the weapons for unexpended rounds. "They're clean," she said.

"I've got bulletproof vests for you," the attendant said. "What other supplies will you need?"

"Issue me a utility knife," Aurora replied. "Maybe a few canteens."

"Sounds like we're going camping," Andrew said, picking up one of the pistols. "I'm not familiar with the

Glock. I wore a Beretta while I was in Iraq. I'd really like the chance to fire this thing before I carry it into the field."

Aurora took the supplies from the attendant. "Thank you," she said. She turned to Andrew. "I agree. It would be a good idea for you and Stefan to practice a bit before we leave."

"Stefan doesn't need to practice," he said. "As a priest he can't fire the thing anyway."

"What do you mean?"

"The Church doesn't allow a priest to serve if he takes a human life. Even if a priest accidentally kills someone, he's out of the priesthood."

"That's a crazy rule, don't you think?"

"No," he said. "You and I both know that burden. I'd like my priests to be clear of it."

"I'm sorry," she said. "I didn't mean to insult your religion. But he has to have a gun, even if he doesn't fire it."

"I hate us having any disagreement," Andrew said. "Last night was very important to me."

She looked at the pistols. "We should not talk about that too much," she stated. "Let's go to the range and do a little practice."

"Lead the way," he said.

Andrew followed Aurora down a hall toward the shooting range.

"Can we have some targets?" Aurora said, entering the room.

"Right away," the range supervisor replied. He stopped momentarily. "Circular?"

Aurora shook her head. "Human form."

"Show me how a Glock works," Andrew said, putting the pistols and vests down on a nearby table.

She slapped a clip of bullets into the weapon and explained how to fire it, including the gun's semi-automatic feature.

Andrew put a pair of ear guards on. "Then let's fire these bad boys off and see how we are."

Aurora put on her gear and raised her gun. She nodded to signal the range attendant. A blaring noise followed.

She fired a single shot and then followed with fourteen rapidly expended rounds.

"Looks great," the attendant said, walking back with the target. "You've put all your shots in the area of the chest. What did you do since you were here last?"

Aurora smiled. "It seems I've gotten over my phobias." She turned to Andrew. "Your turn."

Andrew fired a shot and saw a black hole appear in the left shoulder of the target. He squinted and compensated for the motion he had felt. Fourteen rapid shots followed.

The supervisor walked down range as Andrew cleared his weapon. He returned with the piece of paper, studying it carefully.

"I've never seen shooting like this," he said. "Fourteen shots through a spot less than three centimeters wide, and that's right over the heart."

"I can do better than that," Andrew said. "I'm still not familiar with this gun."

The attendant looked at him. "Who trained you?"

Aurora laughed. "His mother."

They cleared their weapons and then looked at each other.

"This isn't going to be easy," Andrew said softly. "I've gone into battle with many men. But, with the exception of Stefan, I've never gone into danger with someone I loved."

"Andrew, we barely know each other. How can you claim to feel that?"

"I feel. It doesn't have to make sense."

She shook her head. "You're not being fair. We have a job to do, remember?"

He put his hand on her shoulder. "You're right. I'm your deputy from this moment on."

"And I'm in charge of this whole thing. But I don't know what to do next."

He stepped back from her. "You're doing wonderfully. Give the orders, Agent Zamfir."

***

Andrew closed the rear passenger door of the white SUV they had been issued for the trip. He came around to sit beside Aurora, who was in the driver's seat.

She pulled out slowly toward the front security gate. Guards came to attention as the vehicle passed and moved onto the street.

Aurora leaned toward Andrew. "Our first stop isn't that far away," she said softly. "Just up the road is the place he was held for two months before he went to prison."

"Wait," Andrew whispered back. "Are you talking about the place they tortured him? Let's leave that as a last resort."

"Alright," Aurora said. "And let's hope we don't even need to go there."

She negotiated her way through densely congested Bucharest traffic. The view was crammed with advertisements for concerts, movies, and consumer products.

"When did Romania get like this?" Petre asked, studying the various billboards.

"Pretty fast after the Revolution," Aurora said. "You haven't gotten out much?"

"Before today I didn't leave the monastery in fifteen years."

After a half an hour, they had finally cleared the suburbs and were moving at highway speeds toward the north. Green fields of various crops sprawled in every direction, interspersed with random warehouses.

For as many tractors and plows appeared in the fields, there were just as many wagons pulled by oxen.

"Uncle, now that we're out of the city, look outside at the farmland." Stefan put his arm around his uncle's shoulder. "Tell us stories about you and our mother."

"She said you were the weapons expert between them," Andrew said. "What was your rifle accuracy at five hundred meters?"

"What do you mean?" Petre asked.

"How many shots out of ten could you put on a small target, say twenty centimeters, at that distance?"

"How many?" Petre asked with a confused look on his face. "All of them, of course."

Aurora turned her head slightly. "Are you serious? That's really good shooting."

"Do you think you could still do that?" Stefan asked.

"I'm never going to fire another gun," he said. "I haven't fired one since ..."

The three fell silent and let him think.

"Did I ... ?" Petre rubbed his head. "I get so confused. I'm sorry. Sometimes I think things that just make no sense." He fell silent.

"Don't worry," Stefan said. "We're here with you. Spend a little time in those thoughts. You're safe."

After a long pause, Petre took a deep breath. "Since I met you two I've been remembering the last time I saw your mother."

"Tell us what happened that night, Uncle," Andrew said. "Why did she think you had died?"

"We were separated. She broke her arm, so I fell back to take out what we thought were just two people following us. I tried for years to never think of that night, let alone the year I can't remember."

"This is good, Uncle," Stefan said. "Relax and let it keep coming."

"It turned very foggy. Suddenly more men than I could handle surrounded me. I fired my gun in the compromise signal."

"Three rapid shots fast with just the faintest pause between two and three," Andrew explained to Aurora.

"She taught you that too?" Petre asked.

"She taught us everything, Uncle," Andrew replied.

"That was the last time I ever fired a gun. I really wish my last bullet had taken one of them out."

"What happened next?" Aurora asked.

Petre suddenly turned to Stefan. "Can we trust her?" he whispered loudly. "Is it alright for her to know about our operations?"

Aurora smiled at Andrew as they listened to a conversation Petre thought was confidential.

"She's our friend," Stefan said. "We have no secrets from her."

"What's her name again?" he whispered.

"Aurora."

"She's awfully pretty, have you noticed that?"

Aurora looked into the rear view mirror and saw Stefan smiling back.

"She's a very good person, don't you think, Uncle?"

"Can she fight?" he asked.

"I think she'll do okay," he responded.

"Aurora?" Petre said, leaning forward in his seat.

"Yes, Brother Petre?"

"Thank you for helping us."

"You're welcome, sir. It really is my honor."

Petre closed his eyes. "This is difficult. I remember more but ..."

Stefan caressed his uncle's shoulder. "Only if you want to talk about it."

"This just isn't how things were supposed to be," Petre said.

"It's alright, Uncle."

He nodded and sighed. "I knew Doina wouldn't comply with the signal."

"The signal means you assume your partner is lost," Andrew whispered to Aurora. "You get yourself to safety."

"Oh God," Aurora responded. "How do you do that?"

"You're supposed to do it to keep both people from dying."

"Uncle Petre," Andrew said. "You mean to tell us that our mother, who taught us the compromise signal, and the fact that you're supposed to flee immediately, didn't do as she was supposed to?"

Petre leaned forward and put his hand on Andrew's shoulder. "What would you do if you heard Stefan fire the compromise signal?"

Andrew nodded. "I get it."

"So why does this family even have a compromise signal if no one will comply with it?" Aurora asked.

Petre chuckled. "Other Haiduci cells had one. It seemed like a good idea."

Petre sat back and continued the account. "There was this voice, just outside my sight. I could tell he was the leader of the ambush. He kept saying that if I didn't tell Doina to surrender that he would kill us both."

"And that was not an option, of course," Stefan said.

"I knew she was out there and could hear me. I wished so much that I could see her face just one last time. I shouted for her to run away. That's when the voice shot me." Petre was beginning to breathe rapidly.

"Calm down, Uncle," Stefan said softly.

"I have to finish this," he panted. "I shouted one last time for her to flee. That's when everything went black."

Petre was hyperventilating.

"Relax, Uncle," Stefan said with concern. "Breathe slowly."

"I'm going to be sick," Petre said. "I have to get out of this car. Stop the car!" he shouted.

Aurora pulled the vehicle across a lane of traffic and came to a rapid stop at the side of the road. Petre opened the door and got out.

"I'm with him," Stefan said, rushing after Petre.

Petre walked just a few feet off the road and collapsed. Stefan guided him down.

Aurora and Andrew were there just a few seconds later.

"It's a mild state of shock," Stefan said gently, propping up his feet with a few stones.

Andrew knelt down next to his uncle. "I think he actually relived that physically."

Stefan looked at the other two seriously. "He can't handle what we're trying to do here. At what point do we pull the plug on this expedition?"

Aurora crouched down and gently stroked Petre's forehead. "I think we're there right now," she said. "This poor man has been through too much already. I guess we can't expect him to recall events so terrible that his brain blocked them out for forty years."

The three carefully carried Petre back to the vehicle and laid him on the rear seat.

"What's our security plan for when we get back?" Aurora asked the twins, starting the vehicle.

"The two of us will stay at the monastery with him for the time being," Stefan said. "If SRI can provide just an outer perimeter, we should be fine."

"What happened?" Petre asked weakly, fluttering his eyes.

"You passed out, Uncle," Stefan said.

"We're going back to the monastery now," Andrew said. "Just relax there and maybe try to sleep some more."

"Why are you three taking me north?" he asked.

"You don't want to see that area again?" Stefan asked.

"Not really. I'm happy you two came to visit me after all these years, but you still haven't explained how you found me and why a government agent is with us. I know I'm a confused old man, but once upon a time I was a feared fighter. I know how the world works and something very strange is going on. What's really happening here?"

Andrew looked at Stefan and Aurora. "Let's just tell him everything," he whispered.

Aurora nodded approval.

Andrew and Stefan carefully explained all of the events up to that point, as well as everything known about SABIA. Petre asked questions throughout the account that surprised the other three by his grasp of the situation. Afterwards, the old man sat up and looked out the window.

After a long silence, Petre broke into sudden laughter. "Those men did not expect what Doina's sons could do!"

"It was three of them armed and Stefan with apples, Uncle," Andrew said. "They were pretty outnumbered."

Petre shook his head. "And you all really believe that I must be the key to what this SABIA is about to do."

"Even if you're not, Petre," Aurora said. "We have nothing else to go on."

"I am remembering more about that night. Let's keep going."

"Are you certain about this, Uncle?" Andrew asked. "We don't want you to get sick or hurt somehow."

"I risked my life for years fighting the Securitaté. Let me risk it again."

"You're very brave to do this," Aurora said.

"When do you think this attack could happen?" he asked.

"It could be any time," Andrew answered.

"The Staretz told me I would go on a trip to the north today," Petre said.

"One of his dreams?" Stefan asked.

"Yes. And he also told me I would be happy today." Petre leaned forward to get closer to all three. "So far on this trip I've just been scared and confused."

"Are you sure, Petre?" Aurora asked.

He looked out the window and smiled softly. "I'm ready," he said, sitting back. "Let's go see those places. Because, before the day is done, his whole dream will still need to come true."

Chapter Sixteen

The vehicle drove slowly over a rock-covered lane cutting its way through a thick forest. Their first stop would be the house where Petre and Doina grew up.

"We never had more than a horse drawn path to the house," Petre said. "It looks like the current owners haven't added much more!"

"Most of the infrastructure money since the Revolution has gone to the bigger cities," Aurora said. "A lot of these rural areas haven't changed much at all."

They came into a clearing in the trees and saw a small farmhouse. Though clearly old, it had been recently painted bright yellow and was surrounded by extensive gardening.

"Is that it?" she asked Petre.

"It didn't look like a banana when we lived here, but, yes."

"We don't have a warrant that would let us in," she said, parking the car. "But if I identify myself as a government official, I'll bet the current owners will let us see the house."

"Why don't we try to do this less officially," Stefan said. "Do you think the current owners would be willing to let an old monk see the house he grew up in if asked nicely by a priest?"

Aurora laughed. "I see your point."

The group got out of the car and approached the house. A young woman, carrying a baby, opened the front door and stood on the porch.

"Good day," she said. "Can I help you all with something?"

"Madam, my name is Father Stefan," he began. "The good brother here is my uncle, Petre. He actually grew up in your home years ago."

"How wonderful!" she exclaimed. "You must have lunch here."

"I'm embarrassed to have to decline your gracious hospitality, Madam," Stefan said. "We're terribly pressed for time, but my uncle did at least want to see the inside of the house again."

"Certainly," she said. "Look anywhere you would like. I'll get you all a snack ready."

As they entered the house, they were immediately in the kitchen, where the woman was pouring plum brandy into small shot glasses. Handing one to each of her guests, she raised the toast.

"Many years," they all said, clinking their glasses together and drinking the liquor.

"Feel free to explore," she said. "I'll be here in the kitchen for a few moments."

"Thank you," Stefan said, following Petre into the main room.

"When did he live here?" the woman whispered to Andrew.

"Our family lived here for decades. Brother Petre would have left in 1962."

"Do you mean ...?"

Andrew looked at her seriously. "What did you hear about him?"

"My husband and I bought this house just last year. The previous owners told us that a brother and sister once lived here who were arrested for criminal activities."

"That's more or less accurate," Aurora said. "But remember that under communism 'criminal activities' meant anything the government was unhappy with."

"Oh the poor dear," the woman said. "To think that he went to jail for being a monk."

Aurora smiled. "Terrible, isn't it?"

Petre slowly walked through every room of the house, looking up and down the walls. After a long while, he came back into the kitchen where their host had set a table with glasses of mineral water and hastily made sandwiches.

The group ate while Petre told stories of working at the nearby farm collective. They thanked their host and rose in preparation to depart.

"I'm happy you were able to see your house, Brother Petre," the woman said. "Pray for me, please."

"I will," he said, looking around the room again. "There was so much happiness here. This house was filled with faith and love, Madam. Cherish those things and all the rest is easy."

She wiped tears from her face. "Thank you for coming."

"Thank you." Petre kissed her on each cheek.

As Aurora and Petre headed back to the car, Andrew and Stefan stood looking at the house.

"It's funny to think of Mom growing up here," Stefan said. "All we ever knew was the warrior woman. But here she once was a little girl."

"Yeah, but I wish I felt more seeing this place," Andrew said. "For me it's just a house."

Stefan put his hand on his brother's shoulder. "I suppose that's because in all your life, if you're lucky, you have one real house. The one we grew up in there in Wisconsin will always be home for us."

"Even today, most of my dreams take place there," he said. "You're usually in them. Sometimes Mom and Dad. Often in the dream I don't even know they're dead."

Stefan took a deep breath. "The air is sure cleaner here than in Bucharest." He smiled and looked around. "This place is the reason she put us through all that. We hated her for it sometimes, but she was fighting for this peaceful world."

"A place where perfect strangers insist you have lunch with them," Andrew said, nodding.

"A place of brightness in a darkening world."

"May her memory be eternal," Andrew finally whispered.

They started toward the car.

"This whole thing has kept us from really getting any good time together," Stefan said.

"Then you owe me another vacation after this adventure is over."

Andrew opened the rear door and sat next to his uncle. Stefan joined Aurora up front.

"Is there anything else in this area you want to see?" she asked.

Petre turned his head and looked out the window. "I'm not sure."

"That's not exactly a 'no'," Stefan said. "And I take that to mean there's something else around here."

"I could never keep a secret from your mother either," he said.

"And I strangely can't hide them from Andrew. Uncle, where do you want to go next?"

"There was a woman."

"Are you talking about Elena?" Andrew asked.

Petre stifled a sob. "What do you know about her?"

"She was your girlfriend," Stefan said.

Petre continued to look out the window. "And she betrayed us that night."

Andrew and Stefan simultaneously gasped.

"No, she didn't," Stefan blurted. "Our mother once told us her greatest regret was that you died thinking Elena was the leak."

Petre heaved with grief. Andrew put his arm around him.

"Oh, Elena," the old monk whispered.

***

"Thanks for the information," Aurora said, snapping her cell phone shut. "Petre, she's still alive and I have an address. It's not far from here. What do you want to do?"

He closed his eyes. "I've spent forty years hating her because of what I thought had happened."

"You know you need to see her," she said. "So let's just go."

Petre nodded. "Take me there."

Aurora drove through narrow country roads until she pulled up to a small green farmhouse set between a ring of pine trees. An old woman was weeding in a flowerbed in front of the house. The noise of their approaching vehicle caught her attention and she looked up from her work.

"I'll be doing this alone," Petre said.

"Understood," Andrew replied. "Take as much time as you need."

Petre left the car and gently closed the door behind him.

Elena put her tools on the ground and squinted at the black-robed man walking toward the house. She already recognized his gait but strained mentally against the sheer impossibility of it. Despite the white hair and beard, she soon recognized his face as well. She sat down on the front step.

202

"Hello," he said, approaching.

"Petre," she replied.

He bit the long hairs of his mustache and thought about words to use. He finally shook his head. "Elena," he whispered.

They each looked deeply into eyes they had not seen for forty years. These communicated a mutual pain at losing everything that could have been. They swelled with tears.

She wiped her eyes with her hand. "You might be surprised to hear that I've thought about you every day."

"I want to tell you where I was."

"And I want to hear it," she said.

"May I sit?"

She nodded and moved over.

"All those years ago I had kept secrets from you," he said, settling beside her. "My sister and I —"

"I found out later what you two had been doing."

He nodded silently. "I spent years hating you because I believed you had betrayed us."

"I didn't know about it," she said.

He closed his eyes. "And I know that now."

"Tell me what happened to you," she said.

Petre recounted the timeline of his capture and imprisonment and release.

"So why did you become a monk?"

He sat back, starting to relax a bit. "You and I were in school together for fifteen years. Do you remember our Latin class in 12th Grade?"

She looked up to the sky, accessing deep memories. "Catullus."

"Let us live and let us love, my dearest," he quoted.

"Give me a thousand kisses," she added. "You said that the night we were on that hill."

"*Odi et amo*. I hate but still I love." Petre exhaled sharply. "And that's why I became a monk."

Her lips quivered as she put her hand on his shoulder. "The thought of you believing I destroyed your lives — it just tears me apart."

"It wasn't your fault." He turned to her. "We were warriors. We had to think of the reasons our attack had failed."

"Would you have ever let me into that world?" she asked.

"I was going to ask you to marry me," Petre said.

"And I would have said 'yes'."

"And then if God had blessed us with children," he said softly, "you would have learned about it when I began to train them."

She nodded and finally smiled. "So why have you come here today?"

"Doina found her way to America and now her two sons have returned. They wanted me to see these places one last time."

"What do you mean?" she asked. "Are you dying?"

He considered the question and an appropriate response. "Yes," he finally said.

"I want you to know, Petre, that I had a good life."

"In spite of everything, I always hoped so."

"I married and we had five children. I see them and my grandchildren all the time."

"I'm happy you're not alone," he said. "Who's your husband?"

"Constantin Toma."

Petre chuckled through growing tears. "I remember him. A thoroughly decent man."

"He was." She caught herself in a sob. "He made me very happy. And he died just five years ago."

"May he be in a place of brightness and repose."

"And may his memory be eternal," she said.

Petre put his hands on his knees. "I have to get going, Elena," he said.

"I'm grateful that you came here. You've answered questions that have weighed on me for all these years."

Petre leaned over quickly and pressed his lips to hers. She slowly raised her hands and gently caressed his cheeks. They parted and looked at each other through tear-soaked eyes.

A long and lingering moment later, Petre opened his mouth.

She put her finger over his lips. "I know," she whispered.

He smiled, nodded to her, and walked back to the car.

Chapter Seventeen

Aurora turned off the rugged side road and onto a fully paved highway. "Where to now?" she asked.

Petre leaned forward, scanning the forest as she moved slowly down the road.

"Park just past the next bend," he said.

"Where are we exactly?" Stefan asked.

"We can pick up the trail here to the spot where Doina and I hit our last target."

Aurora pulled the vehicle onto the shoulder at the place he indicated. The group started down a gentle slope toward the nearby forest.

"How far from here is it?" Andrew asked.

"About five kilometers," Petre replied. "But this is not easy walking."

"Are you sure you can handle all this?" Aurora asked.

"I'm feeling good," he said.

The three looked at each other and shrugged their shoulders.

"I guess we get to add 'Hiked with an old monk' to our vacation log," Stefan said.

They proceeded steadily through the dense green Carpathian forest. Towering trees stood as proud sentinels all about, spreading a canopy of leaves and letting only a defused sunlight to the forest floor.

"I can sure see how you and Doina were so successful at your efforts," Aurora said. "Anyone who owns terrain this difficult would hold a substantial tactical advantage."

"That was the key to the staff and stones skills," Petre said. "More than once we fought off a group several times our size by using the forest for cover."

"Being able to drop an enemy with a rifle from five hundred meters didn't hurt either," Andrew added.

"True. But the close combat skills provide the discipline needed to acquire the rest."

"I have an idea," she whispered to Andrew. "Brother Petre, can you give me a demonstration of some of your family's close combat skills?"

Petre looked at her curiously. "Alright," he said. "First we need the tools. You boys brought along those pistols, but they didn't have any staves at your headquarters?"

"Sorry, no," Andrew said, looking along the forest ground. "Here's a good candidate." He stooped down and picked up a branch roughly his own height.

"That'll do fine," Petre said. "But all this bark's got to go."

"Why?" Aurora asked.

"Friction in the air," Andrew said, peeling the bark off from the top.

"We'll need some throwing stones," Stefan said, kneeling and collecting rocks from the ground. "Here's a perfect specimen." He stood and held it in the air.

"Oh, it's beautiful," Petre said, taking it from him and examining it.

"What makes it good?" Aurora asked.

"It's smooth and almost a perfect sphere," Stefan replied.

"So what can you do with that thing?" she asked him.

"Pick a target out there somewhere," Andrew said.

Aurora scanned the forest and pointed into the distance. "Alright, do you see that tree just past the big boulder?"

"The tree that's mossier than the ones next to it?" Stefan asked.

"Yes. That's thirty meters away by my estimation. You're saying you can hit that tree?"

"What part of it?"

"Don't be ridiculous!" she said.

"This isn't even a big deal," Stefan said. "The pitcher's mound to home plate is just a little under twenty."

"I'm going to assume that would make sense to Americans," Aurora said.

Stefan laughed and faced in the direction of the tree, pointing his left foot forward. He pulled his arm back. "Five inches above the ground," he said, throwing it in one swift motion.

They all watched as the rock flew toward the target. Moss and bark exploded in a cloud. When it had settled, they saw a mark on the tree near the ground and slightly off center.

"Aw, you pulled it a bit," Petre said.

"I know. I'm way out of practice," Stefan said.

"What are you talking about?" Aurora said. "You threw a rock thirty meters and you're worried about a few inches?"

"A few inches could be the difference between hitting your target or not," Andrew said.

"Or a strike," Stefan said.

"Doina was the stone thrower between us," Petre said. "But even she could miss a target at that distance. Don't feel bad, Stefan."

Stefan smiled. "Thanks."

Andrew had finished stripping the bark off the staff. Petre took it from him and began spinning it around in his hands.

"It's not perfectly balanced, but it'll do fine for a simple demonstration," he said. "Aurora, take the clip out of your gun. Just to make sure we don't have an accident, confirm that you don't have any rounds chambered."

"Understood," she said, checking the weapon as she walked toward him.

"Now re-holster it," Petre said. "And then draw your gun and see if you can get one simulated shot at me."

"No offense, Petre. But if I really wanted to do that, I'm going to run into the woods a bit and come at you from another angle."

"Try it," he said, slipping behind a tree.

She stepped back and took several long strides into the woods. Drawing her gun, she doubled back and came on his position. Not finding him there, she quickly turned around. Petre stepped out from behind a different tree and tapped the staff on top of her gun.

"I could just as easily have knocked that gun out of your hand," he said.

"Or knocked my head off," she added. "That's impressive."

"Imagine two of us coordinating those kinds of moves and also firing guns of our own," Petre added.

Aurora nodded. "Can you teach me some of these things?"

Petre handed her the staff. "All we have time for is Lesson Number One."

Andrew and Stefan both laughed loudly.

"Translated roughly as 'Be the Trees'," Andrew said.

Petre smiled. "There are a lot of specific moves we learn — how to jump between the trees and how to swing the staff. But all of them are built on a simple foundation. Wherever you are, you must know the trees. They're the one true constant of the forest. Then, remember that there is only one thing that you truly control. That's your own body. Your staff, of course, is understood to be an extension of your body."

"This is getting awfully deep," she said.

"Here's what it boils down to," Stefan explained. "Your enemy is fighting in the same forest as you. But they have a different perspective on every tree. With every move you perform, you must make the trees your allies and keep them as obstacles to your enemies."

"How do I do that?" Aurora asked.

"It's more a state of mind toward the trees," Petre added. "Past what we've just said, it can't be taught. It can only be learned."

"Good God," she said, rolling her eyes and smiling.

"God is indeed good," Petre said. "So go out into the forest and see if you can find it."

Aurora looked nervously at Andrew and Stefan. She took a deep breath and started walking slowly into the woods. She wandered around for a while, spinning the staff and jumping between the trees. Finally she headed back.

"I don't get it," she said disappointedly, returning to the group.

"Let it simmer for a while," Andrew said. "It can take some time."

Petre took the staff from her and went into the woods himself. They all watched as he was jumping behind trees and swinging the stick around at imagined enemies.

"He's awfully skilled," Andrew noted. "I think in his prime he was better than either of us ever were."

"That's because he actually fought with these techniques on a regular basis against a determined enemy," Stefan said.

"Maybe even just going through those motions will help him start to remember more," Aurora said.

"Let's keep moving, children," Petre said, returning to them. "We've still got a lot of ground to cover."

Following an hour of slow hiking over rough terrain, they came out of the forest.

"Brasov has grown a bit," Petre said, looking at a sprawl of new constructions. "We still have a kilometer until we reach what was the tree line that night."

"Thank God for development," Stefan said.

The group walked through a zone of newly built hotels and resorts until they reached an older commercial area.

"It's hard to remember where things were," Petre said, pointing his hand in various directions. He turned around and looked up at the large hill behind them. "Alright, I've got it." He crouched down and pointed forward. "It's been completely redone, but that hardware store across the street was the safe house."

Petre sat on the curb and looked slowly over the scene. The three stood near him in silence.

"I took out two men standing guard over there while Doina ran toward the house. I hated that maneuver. If I had ever missed even one target, she would have been running into certain death."

"But did you ever miss?" Aurora asked.

Petre looked up at her and smiled without responding.

"Doina burst in and then I raced to join for back up. She had taken out the enemy by the time I got there. All but one, it turns out."

"What do you mean?" Stefan asked.

"The entire night was a set up. The prisoner we liberated was a plant. If Doina knew that Elena wasn't the leak, she must have also learned that the priest was actually Securitaté."

Petre sat a long while looking at the former safe house. "We shouldn't have done this last attack," he said under his breath.

"You can't think about that now," Stefan said. "You couldn't have known."

"I can't not think about it. This isn't how it was supposed to be."

Aurora sat beside him and put her hand on his shoulder. "You said that earlier. What do you mean, Brother Petre? How should things have turned out?"

"Doina had the dream of becoming a nun."

"She never told us that," Stefan said.

"It's funny how these things cross genders and generations in our family," Andrew said, looking at his brother.

"We talked that night about our future," Petre continued. "I was going to get married and have the family we'd both train in the skills. She was going to be a nun and we'd both die of old age back in that village."

"That would have been a beautiful life," Andrew said. "But you need to know that she lived a good life after she left here."

Petre pushed himself off the ground and stood. "Enough for now. Here is the spot where we finished what we thought was a successful attack. Now it's time to walk in the places where we thought we had made a successful retreat. Follow me, children."

***

"We're almost to the top," Petre grunted, leaning heavily on his walking staff.

Stefan pulled himself up next to his uncle. "You and Mom did this how fast?"

"From the base to the top we usually could do fifteen minutes. That night, however, it was twice that because we were dragging that Securitaté plant."

The four emerged onto the top of the hill.

"Here we are," Petre said, turning around and taking in the whole scene. He laughed. "This is the only place we've been that looks exactly like it did back in '62."

"You and Mom regularly staged here after attacks?"

"Almost always," he said. "We had many escape routes planned off the top here. That night we finally used the one we hoped would never be necessary. Look here," he said, leading them to one side. "Off this eastern slope there's a fissure in the mountain. You can see how it's still lined with pebbles and leaves. We jumped into this and slid all the way down to the main road below. That's where your mom broke her arm. Right after that we were ambushed. And with that, I have finished the story."

Petre sat down, followed by the other three. They caught their breath and felt a cool breeze drying the sweat from their bodies.

"I'm sorry to tell you all this," Petre began. "My memories of that night are as vivid as ever. But there is still a complete block after I got shot. And I feel as if it's unchangeable. I think they did something to me that wiped that year out."

"This was a long shot," Andrew said. "But it was still worth pursuing."

"I agree," he returned. "If for no other reason, I hope this has helped you understand your mother better."

"I feel like such a fool," Stefan said. "I doubted her. And she knew I doubted her. But she was even more of a warrior than we understood."

"She was the greatest there ever was," Petre whispered.

"It wasn't easy growing up with that training," Stefan said. "Uncle, you know that as well as we. Sometimes we resented what she put us through. Well, I resented it more than Andrew."

Petre nodded. "And I resented it more than Doina."

"It was a very difficult and brave thing for her to abandon her own dreams and pass this all on to another generation the way she did," Aurora said.

"I still miss her like this all happened yesterday," Petre said. "When it fell apart on us that night —"

"What did you feel, Petre?" Aurora asked. "Don't tell us anymore about what you did or wanted to have done. Tell us how you felt."

"I want to go back and do so many things differently."

"How did you feel?"

"I felt weak ..." He shook his head.

"You were outnumbered in impossible ways."

"That isn't what mattered. Doina was in danger and I couldn't do anything more to help her."

"You did, though," Stefan said. "You fired off the compromise signal."

"I'm talking about after that. I knew from that moment on, whatever happened to Doina, she was alone. And I was powerless to help her any more. I didn't care about myself. I would have died a hundred times to keep her safe. But whatever happened next, she had to work out on her own."

"This is *Doina* we're talking about," Aurora said. "Are you really surprised that she managed to sneak out of a police state and get to America?"

Petre looked at her and smiled. "You talk about her as if you know her."

"I feel like I do," Aurora said. "She's become an inspiration to me. And I've come to know her family. You all never stop surprising."

Petre got up from the ground. Look, I'm sorry, children," he said. "I wish I could tell you more. There's still a chance that something will come to me, but I think I'm ready to go home now."

They stood up and stretched. Petre looked up through the clearing at a cloudless blue sky.

"Pray for us, Doinitsa," Petre said. He suddenly looked down at Andrew and Stefan. "I'm going to assume that at least one of you has your mother's ears and heard that too?"

"What is it?" Stefan said.

"Get on the ground, all of you."

Petre knelt down quickly. The others followed.

"Listen carefully. About ten men are coming up this hill. Your mother could have given a truer number and their distances. We're under attack here. Tell me quickly, what are our liabilities?"

Chapter Eighteen

"Is this for real, Andrew?" Aurora whispered. "Could it be a post traumatic episode?"

"I don't believe so," he answered.

"One liability, Uncle," Stefan said. "I don't want to lose my priesthood."

"That's not a problem, but you have to give me your gun or we'll have no chance here whatsoever."

"We have another liability," Aurora said. "We have three loaded guns, but no reserve clips."

"Can't we pick up the guns of fallen enemies?" Andrew asked.

"In practice, that's a dangerous thing," Petre replied. "It's distracting and they're frequently empty anyway."

"Mom told us that," Stefan said. "You only scavenge as a last resort."

"And our cell goes hand-to-hand when we run out of ammo, I remember now," Andrew added.

"How could they have found us here?" Aurora asked.

"The easiest answer is that there's at least one more mole at SRI," Petre said. "And someone told SABIA we might come to this hill today."

"Do you have a plan, Uncle?" Andrew asked.

"The closer they get to us, the worse it will be. They'll have us pinned down here and completely surrounded. We need to choose one side and come off it from a position of relative strength."

"Agreed," Stefan said, handling his uncle his sidearm. "Don't forget you can use me for anything non-lethal."

"I've seen what you can do with the stones. There are plenty of good ones up here. Get them quietly."

Stefan began pocketing stones within his grasp.

"I have to think," Petre said. "What —"

"What would Doina do?" Aurora said.

Petre smiled faintly. "We need to do 'The Circuit'."

"We know the maneuver," Andrew said. "For some reason, she made us practice it quite a bit. Give us our orders."

Petre turned to Aurora. "Here's what we're going to do. Going down the chute's not an option. But the chute will provide a natural divider that will let us split the enemy and make them come to us on our terms. We're going to charge down this hill just next to it and take out all the enemy forces we meet on that spot. If we fail at that initial attack, we're done."

Aurora flinched. Andrew saw her and held her hand.

"You can do this," he whispered.

"Stefan, you'll be in the rear. You'll need to stun at least one man as we descend. Otherwise, we won't have the advantage. Obviously anyone Stefan hits still has to be shot dead by one of us, is that understood?"

"Yes," Aurora said. "And I understand that could mean shooting an unconscious man. But this is war."

"They're currently thirty meters down the slope, pretty evenly positioned around," Petre stated. "You see, Aurora, the curvature of the hill will let us deal with just a few men at a time."

"It's brilliant," she said. "And the other men will stop their ascent and start coming around the hill when they hear the gun fire."

"And the ones just on the other side of the chute will be forced to come around the long way," Stefan noted.

"This is a great battle plan," Aurora said. "After we secure our foothold, we can advance around, taking out each person with an element of surprise."

Petre nodded. "Exactly."

"Who made up this plan?" she asked.

"Their father," Andrew said.

"All right, children," Petre said. "Code names only from this point."

"But I don't have one!" Aurora said.

"Your real name would have been perfect." Petre paused as he looked at her. "Alright, you're Minerva."

"The warrior goddess of wisdom," Aurora said with a smile. "You compliment me."

"And you are now officially a member of our Haiduci cell. It's time to fight. There's no time for the whole prayer."

"A place of brightness, Amen," Andrew said.

Stefan, Andrew, and Petre made the sign of the cross.

"On one," Petre said.

They checked their weapons and prepared to move.

"Three, two, one ..."

Petre charged down the hill. Andrew and Aurora followed close behind, weapons drawn. The three dodged around trees as their legs surged through the grass. They knew they were approaching the target and expected Stefan's first volley.

A stone flew over their heads and down the hill. As Petre reached a clearing in the grass, he saw a man in a tan jumpsuit suddenly flip backwards from the impact of a stone on his chest. Petre fired his pistol into the man. Another ran up behind the downed comrade and raised his weapon. A second stone tore through the air above them and cracked into the man's chest. Andrew arrived on the scene and fired into the enemy. They both pulled their pistols across the scene, looking for any further targets. Andrew and Petre heard a gunshot behind them. As they turned toward its source, they saw a third enemy falling to their left. Aurora arrived through a clearing.

"Nice shot," Andrew said.

"Thanks," she replied.

"Second wave is arriving!" Petre shouted, jumping behind a tree.

Andrew and Aurora just found cover when the team heard bullets ripping through the bark all around.

Stefan rushed down to continue his support. He spotted a man coming around the hill, lifting his weapon with a clear shot on Andrew.

"Oh no, you don't," he said through gritted teeth.

Stefan took aim to hurl his stone at the man's midsection. Just as he threw, his foot slipped, shifting the trajectory. He watched in horror as the stone flew and imbedded itself in the enemy's forehead. The man crumbled to the ground.

Petre heard a momentary lull in the action. He raised his hand in the air and pointed in the direction of the approaching enemy. Petre left his defensive position and saw two men step from behind trees. He aimed and fired two shots into each, only to see two more men appear just behind them. The old monk walked steadily forward, shooting at the newly arriving enemy. He fired two shots into each and knew that he had emptied the clip.

"Apollo in descent!" he shouted.

"Castor rising," Andrew called out.

Petre dropped down and rolled backwards. Andrew jumped over him and took his uncle's previous position, firing his pistol at the reinforcements. He moved forward, taking a shot on each arriving enemy just as they saw their fallen comrades.

Stefan twirled from behind his tree and jumped between two of the advancing enemy. They turned to shoot. As the men opened their weapons, Stefan bolted from the spot, leaving the two men to fire on each other's positions. One fell, followed by the other.

"Thanks for teaching me 'The Vice'," he whispered.

"Castor falling back!" Andrew shouted.

"Minerva coming in!" Aurora answered back.

Andrew crouched down and trained his sights forward. Aurora came up beside him and began firing into the arriving line of enemy forces. Andrew took out one more man with his last bullet and crawled back behind a tree.

He saw Petre crouched down and breathing heavily.

"I'm out of bullets," Andrew said.

"Me too," Petre replied. "We'll do hand-to-hand combat from here."

Andrew shook his head. "Minerva has to go down the hill. She doesn't know how to fight this way."

Stefan arrived at their position.

"How are you doing?" Andrew asked.

"Not good," he said. "I ... I killed a man."

Andrew and Petre looked at him with understanding.

"I'm so sorry," Andrew said.

"We can't talk about it now," he said. "What's next?"

"We'll know in a second," Petre said. "Minerva's firing our last bullets. After that ..."

Stefan nodded. "We go hand-to-hand." He took a deep breath. "Nothing matters anymore. I'm a full soldier now. Give me my orders."

Aurora slowly advanced around the hill. She saw a man ahead of her, but stepped behind a tree. Listening for the sound of his steps, she knew where he would be when she jumped out. She spun from behind the tree and she trained her gun on the point. Aurora fired one bullet into his head. Ducking behind a different tree, she heard shots from two guns.

"*Oh my God,*" she thought. "*I understand Lesson Number One! I am the trees!*"

"What's going on out there?" Stefan asked.

"I can't sit here and do nothing," Andrew said. "Give me the staff, Uncle."

"I'm coming with you," Stefan said, grabbing some irregularly shaped rocks from the ground.

Petre sat on the ground, still catching his breath. "I can't go on right now. I don't feel well. Be careful, you two."

Andrew and Stefan rushed in the direction of the firefight. Coming around the hill, they saw two men aiming on Aurora's position. Stefan threw a stone at the one closest to her and then took cover at an adjacent tree.

She heard one of the enemy suddenly gasp. Spinning out of cover, she saw the man doubled over, holding his groin. She fired into him and jumped back to safety.

"Nice shot," she said to Stefan.

"You too."

Andrew charged the second man. Just as the enemy spotted his approach, Andrew slipped behind a tree a few feet away. He looked quickly at the length of his staff and then swung it around the tree, striking the enemy in the face. Stepping out from his cover, he saw the man falling to the ground unconscious. Andrew picked up the man's gun and emptied two rounds into his chest.

"Sometimes scavenging works," he said aloud.

Andrew, Aurora, and Stefan stood in their defensive positions and listened. All they could hear were Petre's footsteps as he approached their position.

"There's no more," he said.

"How many were there total?" Aurora asked.

"I counted fifteen," Andrew said.

"That was more than you originally heard," Stefan said.

"It's not the first time I was off by fifty percent," Petre said.

"Then it's really over?" Andrew asked.

"It's over for now." Petre said.

"And I still have bullets," Aurora said.

Without a word, Stefan began walking back around the hill. The others followed behind.

"Where's he going?" Aurora asked.

"He said he accidentally killed one," Petre replied.

"Oh no," she said. "I know what that means."

They arrived at a clearing and found Stefan crouched next a man, blood still oozing from his forehead.

"I'm so sorry, nephew," Petre said softly.

Aurora reached down and put her hand on the man's neck. "He's still barely alive," she said.

"There's no way to save him," Stefan whispered. "Or my priesthood."

"There's no way to save him," Aurora said. "That much is true." She aimed her gun directly at the man's heart and fired her two remaining bullets into him.

"What are you doing?!" Stefan shouted.

"Now who killed this man?" she asked.

Stefan looked at her with amazement. "I can never thank you enough for what you just did."

"You can live with this?" she asked.

"I don't know that my bishop would completely understand anything I've done today, but ... Yeah, I can live with this."

"Look, we can't act like we're out of danger," Andrew said.

"We can't go back to the car," Petre said. "They probably have a team waiting for us there."

Petre suddenly put his head in his hands.

"Are you alright?" Aurora asked him.

"I don't know," he said.

"Are you hit?" Stefan asked, running his hands on Petre's back and sides. He looked at his hands. "No blood. What are you feeling?"

"We've really got to get off this hill," Andrew whispered to Aurora. "We might have to carry him down."

Aurora nodded to him. "What is it, Petre?"

"I feel very strange suddenly."

"A good night's sleep at the monastery will help you," Andrew said.

"We're not going to the monastery," he said.

"Why?"

"I'll explain on the way. I'm remembering some things."

"Like what?" Aurora asked.

"It's still a bit hazy," he said. "But if I'm right, the attack is tonight."

***

Aurora raced in their new vehicle, a squad car from the Brasov Police department. A passing officer had heard the gunfire up on the mountain and came to investigate. Aurora produced her credentials and informed the officer that national security required them to take his vehicle and weapons. As a siren blared above them, they could see the flashing blue and red lights on the passing buildings. A purple glow was falling over the sky as night approached.

"Let's have it, Petre," she said. "What have you remembered? What's going on?"

"The leader of SABIA," he started. "It's somebody important, right?"

"Yes, and he's well known," Stefan said.

"He wants to take advantage of a massive attack to propel himself to political power," Andrew added.

"That could be any of a thousand people in Romania," Petre said. "What I began remembering a little while ago is what happened in the time immediately after my arrest."

"That's a breakthrough," Aurora said.

"The memories are coming back very quickly now," he continued. "I expect to regain everything."

"That's great," Andrew said. "So what do you know that SABIA finds so dangerous?"

"Something very simple," he said. "A face."

"Whose?" Stefan asked.

"The man who tortured me and eventually gave me drugs to make me talk. He was also the one who shot and captured me that night."

"The one who vanished shortly before the fall of Ceausescu," Aurora said.

"There was something deeply personal between us," Petre stated. "He envied my abilities. In his arrogance, he gave me a split second of opportunity. I nearly choked him to death."

"Good for you, Uncle," Andrew said.

"Well, that only made him so angry that he used the drugs on me. I told him everything I knew. And that's where I also lost a year of memory."

"So his face is what you're talking about?" Stefan said. "Why would SABIA care about you remembering that detail?"

"Because the child has the father's eyes. I'm guessing that, after the Revolution, he began arranging for his own child to be trained the way we were. Our family intrigued him. His money and influence bought his child enough opportunities to achieve great success. And now the child is the one who carries on the father's plan by forming this group SABIA."

"That would seem plausible," Andrew said. "Who are we talking about?"

"SABIA couldn't risk me seeing the similarity, remembering anything, and then connecting all these dots."

"Who is he?" Stefan said frantically.

"It's a she. We saw her on a billboard when we left Bucharest this morning. I believe her name is Vali."

The other three were silent a moment.

Then Andrew laughed. "Vali is the head of SABIA? That's crazy."

"I know," Stefan said. "And you thought she was so hot."

"Petre, this is not exactly what I was expecting," Aurora said. "You're talking about a very famous and popular person. How can you be so sure of this?"

"Think it through the other direction, Aurora. Assuming for a second that Vali is the head of SABIA, she fits the profile perfectly. She's a person of means.

She probably could convert that popularity into votes if she ever went into politics."

"And Stefan noted that she has a remarkably fit body," Andrew added. "Just like someone with our training."

"I seem to remember hearing that observation, not making it," Stefan said.

"Aurora, there's something else we need to insert here," Andrew said. "Vali came to the restaurant that first night you met us. She arrived just after you left. She even came and sat at our table and had Stefan bless a crucifix."

"Well, that must have been very nice for you, given how attractive you think she is," she said with a smirk.

"Aurora —"

"I'm kidding with you, Andrew. It's not for nothing that she's on the cover of every magazine. But her visit to you is a compelling piece of evidence. If she's the one who lured you to Romania, then maybe she couldn't help but meet you the night before she would spring the trap."

"I accept that she fits the profile," Stefan said. "So why do you think the attack is tonight?"

"Don't you see?" Petre said. "The attack is on her own concert."

"There's going to be extra security there. Everyone will go through a metal detector."

"Including the band?" Stefan asked.

Aurora nodded in understanding. "Probably not. My God, this actually does make sense."

"What are we going to do next?" Andrew asked.

"I don't know," she said. "Petre, I'm putting my life in your hands here. How sure are you about this?"

"Vali is his daughter," he replied. "The rest follows logically. But it's still conjecture."

"But you're absolutely certain she's the daughter of the man who tortured you?"

"Yes."

She took a deep breath. "Then let's do this thing. What are our liabilities? Petre, do you have a plan?"

"You're in charge of this one, Aurora. Give us our orders."

She nodded. "Alright, we can't risk SABIA finding out that we know about their attack tonight. And for the time being we can't trust anyone at SRI."

She took out her cell phone and pressed a series of buttons.

"Director Marinescu, please. This is Agent Zamfir and I need to speak with him urgently. Thank you."

She paused and nodded.

"Yes, sir," she said. "Engage the encryption, please." She smiled as she waited another moment. "Are we clear? Sir, we were attacked while taking Petre around. We had just started back, but now he's having some kind of cardiac emergency. I'm rushing him to a clinic in Brasov. Yes, I'll let you know when I have more information. No, we won't be back in Bucharest tonight. Agent Zamfir out." She closed the phone.

"So we're going to stop SABIA's attack without any back up?" Andrew asked.

"The only people I can trust are in this car," she said.

Chapter Nineteen

Aurora brought the car to a sudden stop just outside the security perimeter of the stadium. A short distance past the checkpoint, the concrete walls of the structure were glowing a faint white from the city lights around it. They could hear a booming bass sound produced by the opening act. Even with the concert started, crowds of people were still being processed through the metal detectors.

"If I were trying to produce mass casualties in a stadium," Petre said. "I'd use a bomb. There's probably a place that will look like the logical spot to produce the maximum effect. You three will have to figure that out once you're inside."

"Where are you going to be?" Stefan asked.

"I have to face Vali."

"Shouldn't we face her together?" Andrew said. "If she's the leader of this whole thing, she could be very dangerous."

"Now that I remember her father, I understand better what she's been trying to do. She wants me out of the way. But she wasn't planning on just assassinating me. Even today, those men were trying to take me into their custody alive. She wants to fight me. It's unfinished business between me and her father."

"Why give her that?" Aurora asked.

"Because it's something I need as well," Petre said.

"Alright, follow me," Aurora said, getting out of the squad car and running toward the front of the line.

She pulled out her badge and raised it up to the security screeners. "Official SRI business. I need to bring myself and these three men through immediately."

"Look, I don't know who you are," the guard said. "I can't let just anyone through that flashes a badge. You could have bought that at a costume store."

Aurora looked at Andrew with worried eyes.

"I've got your back," he whispered.

Aurora threw a leg behind the man's knee and pushed him backwards to the ground. She pointed her pistol into his face. "Let me repeat," she said calmly. "I'm an SRI agent and I am taking these three men through right now."

Andrew, Stefan, and Petre went through the metal detector, which began shrieking in response to all their metal accoutrements.

"The concert is cancelled, people!" Aurora shouted to the line. She looked down at the man. "You're just doing your job, I know. So get out of here."

"Yes, ma'am," he said breathlessly, getting up and running into the crowd.

Aurora caught up to the other three as they were reaching one of the stadium entrances.

"Tickets, please," an elderly man at the gate said.

Aurora flashed her badge as the four bounded over the turnstiles.

"Enjoy the show," he said weakly.

The four walked briskly down a darkened corridor. They arrived at an intersection and saw a hall leading to the inside of the stadium.

"This is where we part ways," Petre said. "Once you've found the bomb you'll need to defuse it. Doina taught you bomb-making principles?"

"Of course," Stefan answered.

"Well, bomb defusing is the same science, just in reverse."

Petre looked at Andrew, Stefan, and Aurora standing before him. "I'm so proud of all three of you," he said with a smile. "Be careful."

"You too," Andrew said.

Petre nodded and continued down the corridor.

The other three ran down the hall and emerged to a view of five thousand people packed into the stadium area. The majority of them were wearing green t-shirts featuring Vali's face. The blackness of the night sky was in contrast to the brightly illuminated and packed seats. Various signs and scoreboards rose from the building all around.

They quickly searched the scene. All eventually faced the same direction and squinted their eyes.

"If I were putting a bomb in here," Aurora said, "I would plant it at the base of that largest LCD display on the north corner facing the stage."

"Right," Andrew said. "The shape of the stadium would cause an explosive blowout into the direction of the crowd, and the collapse of the display would add to the casualties."

"And there's no other place in the stadium that would produce the same effect?" Stefan asked, still scanning around. "We may have only one shot at this. We don't want to miss it."

Andrew and Aurora scanned around again.

"I don't see any other place as good for a bomb," Aurora stated.

"I agree," Stefan said. "Let's go."

***

Vali stepped out of the shower in her dressing room. She stood before a full-length mirror and gently rubbed herself with a large white towel. Turning to each side, she studied her body and smiled with approval. She slipped into the tight green dress that was her signature look. As she continued examining herself in the mirror, she heard a knock on the door.

"Twenty minutes until you're on, miss," a voice said from the other side.

"Thank you." She took a deep breath and reached into her purse, removing a cell phone.

"You really do have your father's eyes," Petre said from a chair across the room. He had slipped in while she was in the shower and sat invisibly in a darkened corner.

"Who the hell are you?" she said, turning in the direction of his voice. "How did you get in here?"

"You know who I am. As for how I got in here, the answer is that you made the same mistake three times in one week."

"What do you mean?" she asked.

"You underestimated my family."

She took a few steps toward him. "Yes, I know who you are, Petre."

"But it must surprise you that I know who you are."

"As you said, I have his eyes." Vali looked at the shower room and then back toward Petre. "So did you enjoy the show I just gave you?"

Petre chuckled. "Because of the way my life has progressed, you are the first woman I have ever seen, well, so much of."

"And?"

"As someone said, it's not for nothing that you're on the cover of every magazine."

She put the cell phone down and lit a cigarette.

Petre stood and walked out of the darkness. "Ah, the cigarette again. I'll bet your father told you to do that when you finally had me cornered. It's how he first introduced himself to me. And he thought it would immediately give you a psychological edge in the confrontation."

She grinned. "And it worked. It's called conditioning. Your heart rate is accelerating and you'll lose mastery over your higher mental functions. And in a fight, you'll need control."

"I can see just from the way you carry yourself that you got some significant training," Petre said. "But it wasn't from your father. He was a weakling."

"It doesn't matter who trained me!" she snapped. "I was trained to fight for my family."

"Did he ever tell you I almost strangled him once with just one hand free?"

She gritted her teeth in anger. "I know what happened. And his throat bothered him for the rest of his life."

"He liked having control over helpless things," Petre continued. "You were one of those things as well?"

"Shut up, old man!" she screamed.

"Did I say something to make you lose your emotional balance?" Petre asked. "Remember, in a fight you need control."

She looked at him seriously. "You look older than you really are," she said.

"Prison will do that," Petre replied. "That and killing Communist thugs like your father since I was ten. Thanks, by the way, for giving me the chance to do that again this afternoon. I hope none of those men were your friends. They're all dead."

"I have no friends," she said. She took a final drag off her cigarette and extinguished it in the ashtray. "If you'll pardon me for just a moment, Petre, I have to make a quick call. Then we will continue this conversation."

"Don't touch that phone. I may have been out of touch for forty years, but I'll bet that's how you plan to detonate the bomb. You weren't going to be on stage when it went off. The panic of the crowd might have poured down on you. No reason to risk yourself. So you were always going to set it off during the opening act."

"Old man," she said, "do you really think you can stop me from using my phone?"

"That's why I'm here."

"I'm making this call. What are you going to do?"

"To place that call, you'll have to beat me down. But you're already starting to fear that's something you can't do."

"Why?" she asked. "Because I'm a woman? You think a woman can't beat you in a fight?"

"That insults both of us. Doina was always better than me. But it doesn't matter who your father hired to train you. It's nothing compared to what I can still do."

She huffed. "Then let's do this thing, old man."

***

The three walked briskly in the direction of the hypothetical bomb, trying not to attract attention.

"You know," Andrew said. "It's only a matter of time before security inside this stadium hears about our manner of entrance."

"I may have misplayed that part of my plan," Aurora said. "But in the moment I thought we needed to get in here as soon as possible."

"That's the way these things are," he responded. "You only ever know a thing was a mistake afterwards."

"If it's any consolation," Stefan said, "I think your instincts were correct. I'm seeing a large box placed at the base of that display."

They arrived at the spot.

"It's a bunch of concert programs," Aurora said, leaning over the box. "Petre was right about an inside job. Workers for the show were probably not subjected to security after the building itself was cleared."

Andrew knelt down and began carefully removing programs off the top. He lifted a cardboard divider to reveal several cellophane wrapped blocks. Some electronic equipment was visible between them, with numerous wires across the whole pile.

"We've got a bomb here," he said. "If this is plastic explosives, this thing will kill five hundred people even before this side of the stadium collapses on another thousand." He studied the electronics. "It's a cell phone activated charge," he added. "The IED design of choice in Iraq."

"Could there be a connection between Iraqi insurgents and SABIA?" Stefan asked.

"Doubtful," his brother responded. "There's been so much reporting about those techniques that someone could get a decent schematic for this off a hundred sites on the Internet."

"Don't move!" a voice shouted behind them.

The three turned to see a security guard with gun raised.

"I'm an SRI agent," Aurora said calmly, raising her hands. "We've found a bomb here that needs to be defused immediately. Officer, lower your weapon."

"They told me three terrorists broke into the stadium," he said nervously. "No one said anything about SRI being here."

"We don't have time for this," Andrew whispered.

Stefan took a few steps toward the man, his hands raised high. "Let's just settle down here," he said. "Tell us exactly what you need us to do, officer."

"I need all of you to put your hands up and lay on the ground."

"Aurora, Andrew, we have to do what he says," Stefan said, with a controlling tone in his voice. "Officer, the SRI agent has a weapon, but she's going to set it on the ground now."

"Stefan!" she protested.

"Pollux in ascent," Stefan stated softly.

"Do what he said," the guard barked. "I'll fire this gun if I have to."

Aurora nodded to Stefan, slowly drawing her weapon from the shoulder harness.

The instant Stefan saw the officer's eyes move to her, he bounded forward and brought his foot sharply across the man's face. He crumbled to the ground unconscious. Stefan looked down at him.

"I'm sorry I had to do that to you," he said, taking the man's gun. He walked back over to Aurora and Stefan.

Andrew knelt beside the box and looked up at them. "Do we have something to cut with?"

Aurora produced the utility knife.

"Thanks," he said, taking it from her. "Just so you two know, I've never done this before."

"Then let's hope for beginner's luck," Aurora said, scanning the corridors for more guards.

***

Vali stepped away from her makeup table. "I'm sorry my father isn't here to see me finally defeat you," she said, assuming a defensive position.

"When did he die, by the way?"

"Just three years ago. He had lived to see me hugely successful and SABIA fully formed." She looked at the staff Petre was holding. "Now, I don't have any weapons," she said. "So I want you to lose that stick. I know what you can do with that thing."

"Understood," Petre tossed it across the room into a corner.

"And I can tell you have a gun in the pocket of that black dress you priests wear. Put that away. Let's make this a fair fight."

"I'm not a priest," Petre said, removing the pistol from the pocket of his cassock. He carefully tossed it next to the staff.

Vali immediately dove at her makeup table. Petre charged forward. He kicked her hand just as she pulled a pistol from the drawer. The weapon flew up and hit the ceiling. Vali drew her elbow hard across Petre's face. He fell backward to the floor, stunned by the blow. They each heard the gun land on the floor a few feet away. Petre lunged to the side and grabbed it first, getting up from the ground.

"So much for your fair fight," he said.

Vali snatched her cell phone from the table and quickly pressed several buttons.

Petre raised the gun. "One more move and I will kill you," he said, aiming the gun directly at her head.

"The number is entered," she said. "My finger is on the send button. Even if you shoot me, my hand will clench. I'll bet you sent Andrew and Stefan to disarm the bomb, right?"

"You can't press that button after a bullet goes through your head," he said.

"You're willing to stake Andrew and Stefan on that point?"

Petre said nothing, keeping the gun on its target. His hand began to tremble slightly.

"I still can't believe your sick sister would actually raise them that way," she said. "But SABIA can't have a new generation of Haiduci out there. I'll gladly die for the chance to take them out," she said.

A sharp whistle rang through the room and the phone exploded from her grip. She gasped and shook her hand in shock.

Petre smiled. "A silencer. Nice. But I didn't hear an explosion. So you've failed in your attack plans. You lose, Vali."

"Put that gun down!" she shouted. "I still want that fight."

"Let's see what you have," he said, tossing the gun behind a chair beside him.

Vali rushed toward Petre. Her speed surprised him and he barely blocked a fierce punch she threw into him. Petre lost balance as she unleashed combinations of kicks and punches. He deflected some, but felt his face and stomach pummeled severely.

***

"I don't mean to press you," Stefan whispered. "But I can see a couple of guards down the corridor. They look like they're searching for something. And it's probably us. You may have very little time left here."

"Understood. There are redundant wires all over this thing," Andrew said, studying the contraption. "This is a fairly professional job." He cut wires one by one and then began dismantling the piece more aggressively.

246

"Done," he said, sitting back and rubbing sweat off his forehead. "Add 'disarmed bomb' to the vacation log, Stefan."

They heard the music suddenly stop and saw that people were beginning to move toward the exits. Police officers were apparent throughout the crowd in number.

"I guess word that the concert was invaded by an armed group has leaked out," Stefan said.

"We're going to need to surrender ourselves to authorities or else risk getting hurt," Aurora said.

"It would seem so," Andrew returned.

"Here come those guards," Stefan said, kneeling down. "Let them take us."

"And we still don't know what's happened with Petre," Aurora said, stretching herself face down on the ground.

Andrew and Aurora looked at each other as police officers grabbed their arms from behind and put cuffs on them. They could hear Stefan getting similar treatment nearby.

"You're amazing," he said. "And it's going to be hours or days till I see you again."

"I know," Aurora said. "And I've gotten very used to being around you, Andrew."

***

Vali spun around and brought her foot squarely across Petre's face. He dropped to his knees, then onto all fours. He spit blood and a tooth onto the ground.

She walked slowly back to her makeup table and sat down. Rolling her chair toward him, she put her foot on his back and pushed him to the floor.

"You've inadvertently created a secondary plan for me," she said. "And it's even better than my original."

Pain gripped Petre as his muscles spasmed against several broken ribs. He struggled to get a breath and saw spots before his eyes.

"Listen to how this sounds," she began. "A mentally disturbed monk who was once an anti-communist insurgent has a vendetta against the daughter of the man who captured him. He plants a bomb at her concert and even sends his own nephews to try and disarm it. The plan was to kill his nephews and discredit the poor victim. But somehow I managed to wrestle your gun from you and fire it through the cell phone just before you detonated the bomb."

Petre grunted in pain.

"The publicity I get from all this will help me get elected to parliament on a platform of law and order. From there, everyone discontented with what the new Romania hasn't given them will want me as their president."

He got in one good breath. "And from there, you'll take away freedom," Petre managed.

"Order," she said. "Order is what people want more than freedom."

Petre crawled backwards out from under her foot. He struggled to his feet.

"Please, old man," she said. "You really are finished. Don't make me hurt you any worse. My plan works with you dead or alive. And I'll make you dead if you really want that."

"You're better than I expected," Petre said. "I was wrong to underestimate you."

"Are you seriously still trying to fight me?" she said.

"I'm ready for you this time. You can't land another punch on me," Petre said, almost losing his balance.

"Your choice," she said.

Vali lunged at him. A punch flew forward, but Petre ducked out of the way. He swung his other arm around and crunched his fist through her windpipe. She fell on her back to the floor, grabbing her throat and struggling for a single breath.

Vali looked up at him in shock as her face began to turn pale.

He dropped to his knees beside her. Both their eyes filled with tears.

"God, forgive me for taking life precious to you," he said.

Her eyes blinked rapidly and her eyebrows curled in sadness.

Petre gently set his hand on her cheek. He leaned over and looked into her face. "Lord have mercy, Christ have mercy, Lord have mercy."

Her eyes had gone still.

Petre sat down. "Doina, this isn't how it was supposed to be," he whispered. "Or maybe it was. Those sons of yours ... maybe this was God's plan after all."

He slowly made the sign of the cross. "You can finally rest in peace now, Doinitsa ..." He sobbed once and then took a deep breath. "In a place of brightness and a place of repose."

He struggled to his feet and walked across the room. Petre leaned against the door and gently touched his side, feeling something swelling rapidly within.

"I had hoped to tell you in person," he said out loud, struggling to breathe. "It was an honor to fight beside you."

Petre slid slowly down the door to the floor. With a faint smile on his lips, he closed his eyes.

Chapter Twenty

Aurora hesitantly pulled on the heavy wooden door of a downtown Bucharest church. Her eyes were accustomed to the brightness of the late spring day and so she saw next to nothing in the darkness inside. She stood for a moment to let her eyes adjust.

"Can I help you?" a voice said off to her right.

"I'm here to light a candle," she said.

"They're one *leu* for three."

She chuckled. "Why do they cost next to nothing?"

"We don't want anyone in need to be impeded from an important prayer. I give them away for free if I think someone can't afford even that."

Aurora was now seeing the outline of the room and spotted an old man seated behind a table with boxes of candles in front of him. She approached him and set a twenty *lei* note on the table. "I'll take three, please," she said. "Keep the change for the people who can't pay."

"Bless you," he said, handing her three brown beeswax candles. "You seem new to this."

Aurora looked at him and nodded. "Yes. I lit my first candle just yesterday."

"This must be very serious for someone so hesitant in her faith."

Aurora did not know the reason, but she felt a strong need to explain the situation to this stranger. "My friend isn't expected to live. And even though I'm not a believer, I can't just sit and do nothing. So here I am, Father."

"I'm not a priest," the man said. "I'm not even a monk. I'm just a man who volunteers in the parish."

She nodded silently.

The man smiled. "You're SRI, aren't you?" he asked.

She laughed aloud. "How would you deduce that from looking at me?"

"I know a few things," he said.

"You got me," she said. "Can you show me where I go?"

He stood from his table and picked up one of the candles. "Come with me."

Aurora walked behind the man as he proceeded quickly up the center aisle of the Church. He leaned over and kissed the central icon and then stepped to his right. He stood beside a tray of sand and lit his candle on one already burning there.

"Why do you volunteer here?" she asked.

He looked at the candle he had just lit. "I have a lot to atone for."

"So do I," Aurora said.

"For your friend," the man said, crossing himself. "May he be healed and prosper for the remainder of a long life."

Aurora stepped up beside him. She lit her own candle off his and set it in the sand. "I still don't know if I believe in any of this," she said.

"That's alright," he replied. "A new faith has to start somewhere."

***

Andrew sat beside Petre's hospital bed. Stefan stood nearby, looking out the window at a traffic jam below.

"I think he's waking up," Andrew said.

Stefan came to the bed to see Petre fluttering his eyelids.

"Where am I?" he mumbled.

"You're at a hospital in Bucharest," Stefan said. "You had emergency surgery on a whole lot of things Vali messed up inside you. It looked pretty bleak for a while, but now they say you'll be fine."

"You stopped the attack?"

"You stopped it, Uncle," Andrew said. "They think the bomb was useless without that cell phone."

"Where's Aurora?"

"She's out praying for you," Andrew said. "Ever since I showed her how to light a candle and kiss an icon in the chapel, she's been hitting all the local parishes."

Petre chuckled, but then winced in pain.

There was a faint knock at the door and then it opened.

"May I come in?" the Staretz asked, poking his head through.

"He's awake and I'm sure would love to see you," Andrew said.

"How do you feel, Brother?" he asked.

"I feel terrible, but they tell me I'll live." Petre smiled at the Staretz. "And this isn't what you expected, is it?"

The Staretz sat down in the chair beside the bed. "I'm happy to see one of my dreams not come true for once."

"What about SABIA?" Petre asked.

"With the information they found in Vali's house, they've basically taken the organization apart," Andrew said.

"She was the organization," Petre said. "Without the head there really wasn't a body. And was there another SABIA mole at SRI?"

"Marinescu's secretary," Stefan said. "But you just need to concentrate on getting better, now. There will be time to explain all the details to you later."

"But it's over?"

Andrew smiled. "It's over."

***

"I propose a toast," Andrew said, standing from a restaurant table. "To the toughest monk in any Church, our beloved uncle, Brother Petre.

The guests all stood in turn. They filled a private room at the restaurant where Andrew and Stefan had dined their second night in Romania. Around one large wooden table everyone with a connection to the struggle against SABIA raised their glasses.

"God grant you many years," Aurora said, clinking her glass against the others.

"Good health, Uncle," Stefan said.

People began sitting down.

"I have a presentation to make," Director Marinescu said, remaining standing. "As the only person here who actually belonged to the Securitaté that Petre fought, we were once technically enemies." Director Marinescu took a blue velvet box from a pocket of his suit coat. He opened it and lifted a silver medal with a ribbon in the blue, yellow, and red of the Romanian flag.

"Petre, if you would do me the honor of please standing ..."

Petre stood up and turned hesitantly toward him.

"We at SRI have been awfully busy the last couple weeks," Director Marinescu began. "We've dismantled what was left of SABIA. And now we're happy to take a break and honor the man who saved Romania from destruction. Only a few times since the Revolution has SRI bestowed its highest recognition of valor. It has, of course, never been given to someone who wasn't an SRI agent. But as director I feel these circumstances warrant it. For your critical service to a grateful nation in the area of national security, I hereby award you,

Petre Rădulescu, with our Medal of Honor." He put the medal around the monk's neck.

The group applauded as Petre shook the director's hand.

"I accept this in the name of my entire family, living and dead," he said.

"I know tomorrow you're receiving the Romanian Star from the President himself," Director Marinescu said. "But I wanted to do what I could."

Petre lifted the medal and looked at it. "I'll receive that graciously as well. But there's something about me receiving the highest award of the Securitaté that seems somehow more meaningful."

The director turned back to the group and faced Andrew and Stefan. "I have no authority to bestow anything on two American citizens," he said. "And I have to admit I didn't like your involvement in this case at all. But that's because at the time I didn't understand just what you two are. All I can do is offer you my deepest thanks for risking your lives to protect your ancestral land."

"Thank you," Stefan said.

Agent Williams raised his wine glass. "I don't have anything to bestow on them either, except to say that I'll be happy when they've cleared Romanian airspace so I can stop cringing every time the phone rings."

Aurora smiled nervously and looked across the table at Andrew.

"Give me a call," Williams said in a low voice to Andrew, handing him a business card. "The National Security Agency could really use someone with your talents. I know someone there who could move you through the hiring process pretty fast."

"Thanks," Andrew said. "But I have other plans." He set the card down on the table.

"I have one more recognition to give," Director Marinescu said. "When I assigned her to this duty, Agent Aurora Zamfir seemed a bit hesitant at first."

Aurora looked at her boss nervously.

"What she has accomplished can only be described as performance way above and beyond the call of duty. And I hereby promote her to the rank of Senior Investigator. She is at once the youngest and first woman to achieve this rank at the SRI."

Aurora looked at him seriously. "Thank you, sir," she said.

"Well, we can't thank you enough," he said. "At a crucial moment in the investigation, we could have lost everything if you had not stood your ground against me. I look forward to great things from you in the future."

Waitresses arrived with several plates of food. Other wait staff refilled the glasses and left carafes of wine behind.

"We could spend the whole night talking about this," Petre said. "Let's just eat and drink and enjoy the evening, my friends."

The group celebrated into the night. The Staretz and Petre returned to the monastery at eleven. Andrew walked Aurora to the street when her SRI transport was arriving.

"I've wanted a moment alone with you all night," he said. "I know you've been busy, but I've hardly seen you since we foiled the attack."

"Andrew," she said, looking into his eyes. "I don't know how do to this kind of thing. To say we've been through a lot together would be a ridiculous understatement."

He smiled. "Indeed."

A black Mercedes pulled up to the curb. An SRI agent got out of the front passenger seat and opened the rear door for Aurora.

"What is there to say?" she asked.

"That's the thing," he said. "I've accepted an offer to teach Latin —"

"Good," she interrupted. "That's what you wanted and I'm happy for you."

"Aurora," he continued. "I'm going to —"

"Good luck, Andrew," she said. "We'll always have our memories of a sweet time when we —"

Andrew put his finger on her lips. "I'll be teaching Latin at the British Academy here in Bucharest."

Her face fell. "What?"

"I'm staying," he said, looking into her eyes. "What did you think I would do?"

She shook her head. "Andrew, you heard the promotion I just got."

"I know!" he said. "It's wonderful. You've gotten everything you wanted and everything you deserve."

"I can't be involved with a non-Romanian citizen," she said quickly. "That's how it is with security clearances."

He retreated a step and looked at her. "The nephew of Petre Rădulescu counts as a non-Romanian?"

"Yes." A tear rolled down her cheek. "I'm sorry, Andrew."

He opened his mouth to respond and realized there were no words that could change things.

"I am too," he said softly.

A silence hung between them, neither knowing how to walk away. Andrew finally closed his eyes, tears of his own now flowing.

"SABIA is gone now," he whispered.

She threw herself at him and kissed him deeply. The two clung to each other and all their lost dreams. He broke away first.

"You have a good life, Aurora," he said, turning and walking away quickly toward the restaurant.

She shook her head as she watched him climbing the stairs toward the door. "This isn't how it was supposed to be," she whispered. She got in the car and closed the door.

Andrew spun around suddenly and watched her vehicle speed away. As he turned back around, he saw his brother just inside the restaurant.

Stefan walked slowly toward him.

"You can tell what just happened?" Andrew asked.

"Yes," Stefan said, pulling his brother into an embrace. "I know."

The brothers cried together and found themselves mourning much more than the current moment. They were burying their parents, lamenting lost years, and fearing an uncertain future.

"Let's go back inside," Andrew said, putting his hands on his brother's shoulders.

Stefan nodded in silence.

The twins returned to the table the group had held.

"Not that we need it," Stefan said to a waitress, "but please bring us some more wine."

The waitress returned with two glasses and a carafe of red wine. She filled them and departed.

Andrew picked up the card Agent Williams had given him.

"You're going to call him," Stefan said.

"I know," Andrew replied, looking up at him. "After all we've been through I still need a job when I get home."

"And becoming a spy would seem a good fit for you."

Andrew chuckled. "Yes, because the only things I know how to do are teach Latin and fight wars. And I just lost the love of my life."

Stefan sipped his wine. "I talked to Kristie and John earlier. We're coming back here in just a month so they can meet Petre."

"I'll see if I can join you."

Stefan nodded. "Good. I still owe you a vacation without gun battles."

Andrew's eyes glistened with tears. "I don't know where any of this is headed."

"We'll never be far apart again," Stefan said. "Not in any of the ways that matter. Just find what gives you purpose."

Stefan raised his glass and poured some wine onto the table. Andrew did the same.

"For the dead," Stefan said. "May their memory be eternal and may they find rest in that place where suffering and sorrow are no more."

"May they rest in a place of brightness and a place of repose," Andrew continued.

"And for the living," Stefan said. "According to your will, O God, assist us in our efforts so that we can create a world in which peace profound reigns."

"Amen," they said together.